Three enclosed illustrations originally appeared in *Live Through This*, published by Seven Stories Press.

Library of Congress Cataloging-in-Publication Data

Road, Cristy C.
  Bad habits : a love story / Cristy C. Road.
    p. cm.
  ISBN-13: 978-1-59376-215-5
  ISBN-10: 1-59376-215-1
  1. Graphic novels. I. Title.

PN6727.R555B33 2008
741.5'330670869209747I—dc22

                              2008017342

Cover design by Alvaro Villanueva
Cover illustrations by Cristy C. Road
Interior design by Cristy C. Road & Alvaro Villanueva
Printed in the United States of America

Soft Skull Press
An Imprint of Counterpoint LLC
2117 Fourth Street
Suite D
Berkeley, CA 94710

www.softskull.com
www.counterpointpress.com

Distributed by Publishers Group West

10 9 8 7 6 5 4 3 2 1

BAD HABITS

A LOVE STORY

by Cristy C. Road

· SOFT SKULL PRESS ·

·BROOKLYN ·

*This book is dedicated to the discounts at the grocery store,
Coney Island, short lines in public restrooms,
organic lube, and proper communication.*

CHAPTER ONE

The first step
is always disillusionment.

As the clocks ticked timelessly and the humans aged blindly, every antique corner of New York City was in danger of destruction. But when I looked outside my window, every color and virgin texture of her condemned ruins took me someplace beautiful and far off.

Like that one corner on Graham and Siegel—its perfectly painted signs and boots kicking a perfect cloud of distressed concrete. I liked old painted signs the way other people liked the *Mona Lisa* or pornography. The voices on that strip would seep into one of my ears, and out the other, lyrically, in my grandfather's tongue. I wanted to caress those corners. But indignantly I asked questions that I would rather not have had to ask: *Will everyone stop speaking Spanish when the rest of Brooklyn is derailed?* and *When will the bricks burn and resurrect as sleek, pure architectural malice?* or *Who's gonna save the souls of the cobblestone sidewalks and brownstones doused in accidental ivy?*

Something better save us now, I thought, *so my kids can know what I know.*

★   ★   ★

And, like Brooklyn, the human heart is divided into several humble portals, each with a function, relevance, history, and culture distinct to its region. Every developmental blow cripples the antiquity of its boroughs, and every imperfect experience cripples the wellbeing of every corner of the heart. But the city doesn't stop, and the human heart trudges with clandestine motivation.

However, in those safe havens and hidden opportunities for wayward glory, the human heart beats to the rhythm of a sick, sick world.

This is a love story. It all started when I broke my roommate's bong. Actually, I'm lying. It may well have started in 1997, after I learned I was bipolar and did too much speed. The chaos flourished after I kissed this one girl in some raver's house party in west Miami, and the rumor mill toppled my campus hallway. The party was at Victor Castellano's house and I can't remember a day I haven't thought of the smell of his stucco ceiling. Lead poisoning, I think. Or maybe just because on that day, I learned being Latin, bisexual, and sexually unkempt was clearly undesirable.

I live in a country where earthly mental enhancers are outlawed, because the crops are owned primarily by people with a heritage other than that of our leaders. Fortunately, I would sometimes soar atop an otherworldly pillar on which the unorthodox was celebrated. In my country, humans are taught to think that no worthwhile knowledge can come from the vices they consume in order to salute their good bearings—or maybe get over damaging pasts, where behaving badly is the only choice that could alter them. I wanted to find compelling morals in my misfortune, but until now, I've just found shit.

I'm as imperfect as anyone else, with a self-esteem more bruised than a smoke-infested lung. But it seemed like I could make it out alive, whether or not that involved crawling out of a puddle of my own blood, with only a little white flag to signal friends. Attempting change made sense after moving to this city, with its history and future penetrated both by savvy rebels and conservative maniacs.

Who would have thought that the country that tarnished home-cooking with delightful items like Hot Pockets in order to make the life of a pothead that much simpler, would be so unqualified at understanding the existence of different, or rather, real people? I fumbled, until defying rules became second nature to me.

Truthfully, though, existing in America with an alternative lifestyle hardly means immunity from injustice. New York City, alternative in it-self, had several faces of good, evil, rich, and poor long before I got here. And while plenty of independent people with independent minds plaster sidewalks and signposts with words and images in hopes of preserving any culture outside of the white-bread basket of glass condos, diversity disap-pears, and men still rule.

Why die? I thought, counting the times I've hated being alive. *I'm a ticking time bomb, I guess. I'd rather just act upon my anger.* To a conservative many, I was the scum of the earth, and my allies were just numbers. To me, we were the things that went bump, crack, and hump in the night.

CHAPTER TWO

Mercury had been in retrograde
for like, half a year.

AUGUST

I t was the end of the summer, right after I fled the confines of my hometown of Miami, Florida. New York City resonated with the feeling of a gaudy Friday night without any cozy thresholds at arm's reach. It's drenched in what, conventionally, would be bad taste; even after the ethnic and class-based cleansing of thousands of New York City businesses. Upon moving, I was afraid of what a city would look like after the recent mayor swept off its homeless with the same carelessness one would display in sweeping horseshit. However on that summer, I preferred to just sit there and blind myself to destruction. I focus a lot less on the condominiums swelling the cost of living while manic and determined to live a new life. In the end, my vision of New York was often clouded by prosperity, so moving in was still a dream, despite reality's occasional visitation.

A little east of a bar I was working at on 2ND Avenue, Isabelle had an office, a Bichon Frise, and a disarray of toddler toys on her carpeted floor. Two doors down was Lorenzo, a man with a restaurant that had been standing there since the Vietnam War. On the opposite side lingered Bob, a Vietnam vet who asked me about the South when I sat on a cast iron bench, waiting outside of Isabelle's office. Like my favorite corner on Graham and Siegel near my post office in Brooklyn, a bright side can often startle you, like déjà vu. After my shift, I would stumble, in a drunken sweat, toward Isabelle. We would share a spliff, a hippie concoction of St. John's wort and red wine, and a half-trifling prediction.

Isabelle's ceiling was low and tulle, and gold tassels hovered festively above my head. Rooms with low ceilings always made me feel wiser because I felt several feet taller. Isabelle was gonna give me a tarot card reading.

I always believed in astrology because if something went to shit, I could then blame a psychic-gone-bad instead of my failing intuition or dead-on stupidity.

"I feel like shit. I need to change my life."

"We'll see what the cards say. And then we'll see what you can do."

"It's just so much easier to ignore the reasons for my loose ends. I'd rather just know the future." I was terrible at reasoning. She flipped the last card and looked at me with a maternal assurance.

"Can it."

"Ugghhh."

She spoke with an irritating glee that suggested sentiments of *I told you so* or *shut up and get over yourself.* Despite this, I adored her and appreciated harsh criticism and motherly wisdom.

"Great. Not another mind-fuck. Or a reminder that all lovers take after my biological father or my worst fucks."

"You can love something besides—"

"I won't fuck a sheep, Isabelle. Or any randoms at the bar tonight. Those are the worst. A shitty one-night stand, or a good one I inappropriately fall in love with."

"No! Go fuck! Fuck fuck fuck." I walked towards her arched corridor that faced a lingerie store on 2ND Avenue. It displayed a perfectly sculpted orange torso that reminded me of Tatiana, the last person I thought I might have loved.

I walked outside to smell the air of barbecue, street fair, and skin-prickling squalor. Beside me, two teenage punks embraced under the sputtering fluorescents of a tattoo shop. Pedestrians smiled, farted, sneered, and scrutinized in unison.

That night I searched for new scandal. I'd fought off unfortunate drug binges and heartless interactions for most of the year. Outrage was my second nature, but I wanted to transform it into passion the way I wanted most of New York City to transform into a delicate visual of who she once was. We were kindred spirits, New York and I. The world as we knew it intensified our toxicity, but from our loose pockets we often broke out champagne. *And in another five years*, I thought, *we may be back to pure fire.*

I got on Dorothea, my makeshift BMX, and rambled through town with a desire to run away from something much faster than an SSC Aero, the only existing car that can go 257 miles per hour.

"It's you that I love, New York City," I told every roving strip of concrete. "And maybe one day you won't be so reconstructed, and maybe I won't feel so post-war."

CHAPTER THREE

My first love blew.

I'm a Cuban-American. Tradition, to most of us, was common sense. I grew up in a neighborhood so Cuban I thought white people were fictional characters on film and television. That is, until one day when I was four years old, wandering through the walkways of some amusement park, and there they were. I learned English around the age of four, in order to start public school in the United States. Unlike my siblings, I lost my accent around my teens, perhaps because I was always a loner, with no Cuban companions to influence my developing epiglottis and vocal folds. The first voices I began mimicking were those of angry (mostly American) punk rockers, who were perched inside my headphones. I blame them.

Like most humans, misfortune pissed on me periodically throughout life. I adapted to financial or social restrictions through casual acknowledgement, because I was a relatively aloof kid. I was okay with my life, what it did and did not entail, although I always seemed to overanalyze and criticize the situations that pained me. Evidently, my mind appeared clearer while swimming in my own piss.

* * *

The *quinceañera*. It's the Latin counterpart of the sweet sixteen, embellished with strict rules. In the ceremony, the newly-fifteen-year-old girl dances with her father while fifteen couples encircle them in song and dance. I didn't have a father, didn't have fifteen friends with fifteen partners, and felt uneasy at the thought of wearing a gown in public.

My family was devastated for several months, but I opted against the *quinceañera*. Instead of it, the money saved went towards a sonic blue Fender Stratocaster. The energy saved was invested in second-rate porn and learning the chords to "Kabuki Girl" by the Descendents on my new axe. Adolescent years make or break a person, I thought. I often think something broke me so painstakingly that I wouldn't have given up the spoiled results for anything.

I rapidly grew toxic, like old bread mold in the hottest days of August. As the black sheep of the family, I bore the traits not of the women who raised me, but of my biological father. A gas problem, peculiar tallness, bizarre health issues, an inherited tan, an unwillingness to be quiet, even when specifically requested. Disheartened, I nevertheless made constructive use of my genealogy and made the most of the one inherited desire I wasn't disillusioned by: the need to flee irresponsibly and become some kind of starved artist; in my case, a writer. As a kid, I was relatively uninterested in knowing about my father, so I never really questioned the lack of information I was given

in regards to his existence. So I said, *Fuck him, I'm just special*— at least when placed within the circumference of my relatives who actually loved me.

At sixteen, I began to mistake myself for a twenty-five-year-old man. I was campy and high-stress. I hooked up with older dudes and studied *Roget's Thesaurus* on the toilet to develop the dialect of a tortured old sailor. I felt post-pubescent self-love. I wanted to stay sixteen—so I did, perhaps until I turned eighteen. Then, I spent all my anger on creating towering defenses against patriarchy, only to realize that hiding vulnerability only created more baggage. Punk rock music and the revolution of everyday life was all that mattered—and to pay the bills, I just took some naked pictures. Cementing my face to the speakers of a record player, my defenses stated punk rock and a little bit of speed were all I needed to stay relatively sane.

But people—unfortunate bosses, dishonest friends, and the guy taking the naked pictures—were burning me as the fire in my soul was peaking. As I started to acknowledge my inability to face a lot of looming conflicts, that utopian vision of punk rock, girlhood, and autonomy was tarnished. For once, I was capable of murdering someone. Aside from growing up, I started feeling a peculiar disconnection from my culture. Eventually, I re-invested in Cuban music and literature to relearn where the fuck my natural idiosyncrasies even came from.

*   *   *

After a day or two of amphetamines running aimlessly through my nostrils, coming down simply fast-forwarded my noradrenalin, the hormone conducive to anger. This anger clarified the reasons behind what thwarted my self-esteem, reasons I often denied. After a splurge of self-hate, the numbing revelations would begin, and I'd ask myself: *Why is love harder than heartache?*

At eighteen I attended a college in South Florida. I had tried cocaine through most of my college years, and to me it was almost the same as speed. Marvelous and horrendous. But it assisted with the ever-so-turbulent cycles of both self-esteem and human interaction.

Through my life I've watched love disintegrate inexplicably, like with my father who left when I was, I guess, nine or ten. And like with my first real friend who decided her boyfriend and his friends were better than me. Watching the wounds form wasn't too much of a problem. As a kid I was quick to dust off conflict. In college, I began realizing how those wounds transformed into scars. Eventually, the truths burned me.

*   *   *

During those years, I was entering a more fragile, baffled state of existence. Nothing was right—class, race, war, gender, men, women, animals, law. When I was twenty, I met a paradox named Randall. Randall was both a buzz kill and a redeemer.

*   *   *

Randall had the language of a suave composer and used it to his—and undeniably only his—advantage. Randall hopped trains, wore scuffed boots, and adored wrecked girls with aimless destinations. I related once and we became two young, tortured souls who questioned society and authority before questioning one another.

Randall was the kind of man who could swear he felt the beating of some girl's heart from a mere glance of her eyes beneath a slush of rain and moonlight. I spotted him at a punk rock show in a town not far from Miami a little before my twentieth birthday, and soon enough, my emotions were fried. Love at first sight was unstoppable. Randall was a world traveler and lived in Florida for weeks at a time, with the occasional regional hiatus. We wrote letters, traveled the country, and took things with intentional speed. Flawless chemistry paralyzed our conversations, observations, and making out.

Then we tried to have sex. When we tried to have sex, I remembered that feeling of hormonal balance and human intimacy as less of an avalanche than usual—all of a sudden, sex was difficult, even in comparison to the time I lost my virginity in a public bathroom of a punk show. Sex with Randall was peculiarly unbalanced. Seeing eye to eye didn't seem possible when we were naked. Throughout all this I held my breath. It was so much simpler to fuck, run, and forget until we met again. So I did just that.

Randall and I met as I had begun to violently resent the actions of men who had tried to fuck me, whether or not I was dry or asleep. I was entering a period of productive anger. Inside, I wanted to murder these past lovers, but instead, I discussed male socialization and politicized gender dynamics with Randall. Entering my twenties meant rising up in a feminist fashion unknown to my teens. I became a relatively serious human rights activist, working and talking about violence, rape, and things I mostly wanted to end. Eventually, I learned I was still beset by weaknesses I wanted to alter. Starting to understand that the human experience is globally imperfect, I also began to question the romantic inadequacies that existed between me and Randall.

In an apartment in Miami, during a later period of our romance, we had woken up in a putrid heat, where human sweat and fluid coagulation was a natural and predictable circumstance. Randall's fingers were inside of me, but my internal juices weren't flowing at a graceful pace.

"Gross," Randall exclaimed. That morning I hated sex, but I hated my body even more.

The moment defined our sexual relationship, which was built on an im-balanced arsenal of insults and tactlessness. Randall never laid an aggressive hand on me; he just made me feel terribly ugly, classified me as wrongly equipped—my organs were too small, too dirty, too dry, or too mysteriously trapped beneath a miniature hood of flesh he didn't even want to deal with. Randall would try to fuck me; I would decline. I was dry and my organs were exhausted, but he would ask more and try harder. After all, my insides,

after being taunted, weren't built to be accepting of horrendous phalluses. I lay hurt, sick. My feelings for him, otherwise, coexisted with regret. I learned Randall's Achilles heel lay between his legs and pulsated at a deplorable rhythm orchestrated by his lack of interest in knowing his lover's body even as little as he knew his own. Randall's gigantic penis was a curse.

My first instinct after violation was this—spark up a blunt, put on a Green Day record, take a shower that could well last an entire day, forget anything ever happened.

I was terribly infatuated with the idea of this lover whom I wished would love me in return. And my attraction to Randall's constant emulating of my favorite writers typically blurred the fact that I couldn't trust him. That's the case with a lot of vaginas: Their inability to moisten in the face of coercion is often ruled by any skepticism towards the coercive partner, rather than biology. But it's those moments—when our naked bodies strain against expected behavior, when we see the way we look and the size of our hands—that dictate who speaks loudest and who cowers into the most introverted corners of the subconscious. I loved Randall when we talked on public transit, but he made me feel like a train wreck when my clothes were off. Overall, I wish I knew he was capable of such bullshit when this started.

I didn't choose to let sex like that drag on, but I had fallen in love before any damage started. Our break-up entailed a series of quarrels in which I cried and yelled, and Randall stared, fidgeting on a guitar. I felt utterly worthless; truthfulness proved to have no bearing. So, in the spirit of what I inherited, I left Randall. I left him and went back home with new, unwanted baggage. From then on, it took more than a fresh romance to awaken my internal muscles. Admitting anything, ever, made me feel wrong, and the possibility of having to explain my past to anyone felt both scary and annoying. That openness would have to involve some kind of love, anyway. And while believing in love and vaginal penetration sat on a shelf with other dented experiences, I just went on with the rest of my life.

CHAPTER FOUR

I don't care if you referenced
Emma Goldman in your 'zine,
I still think you're full of shit.

I t's been over a year since that fire went out. But in my body lay the damaged ends of so-called damaged goods that I had avoided tending to for too long. I don't feel any guilt for discarding such things—there is a time for everything. My impulses to clear the smoke came few and far between—for me at least. That fall, the intent to master the art of *getting over* felt appropriate. Randall, Dad, and dry towns were all beating at my chest in unison as I stepped foot into 2G, my first apartment in Brooklyn. I'm terrible at pacing myself—the human art of growth was hardly a little jaunt through life for me, but an avalanche that appeared at my door, condensed and uninvited.

*   *   *

I had ventured to this city of smokestacks and fire escapes in order to find the spiritual enlightenment one can't get from palm trees. En route to New York from Florida, I had waltzed through Philadelphia, Baltimore, Boston, and DC like a hen with her head cut off; a hen that evidently died in Brooklyn. 2G was an underdeveloped loft with exposed pipes that occasionally pissed sewage onto unsuspecting tenants. I compromised, accepted the architectural decay, and enjoyed living there for a minute—until I ended up being too loud and obnoxious for the ambiance. During my time at 2G, Tatiana, an old flame, said distance had become too vast, and she would much rather be friends. We had a gorgeous friendship and only had been physical a few drunken times, but whatever. I guess I was one of *those crazy people*—I just lived in denial. I fled this heartbreak and convinced myself the fires would return, whenever I saw her again.

But Tatiana wasn't what truly burned me. The same week, I learned Enrique, the guy who scraped me off my more worthless teenage habits, died of a heroin overdose.

After I fled the cul-de-sac of tender sores, I went on a cocaine bender for a spiritual lift. I attempted to force happiness, but couldn't find medications whose effects wouldn't clash disagreeably.

Then I answered a telephone call from my friend, Spike. His housemates had brought home several injured pigeons and he discovered a girl with a wrecked soul would be much more fun to live with than sick waddling pigeons. Soon, I took a spot in his apartment. I really loved and admired my friends at 2G, but as they brewed pots of coffee at 6 AM for school, yoga, and the law firm, I blew rails off the kitchen counter. I knew living there would produce a harvest of significant problems.

I didn't rid Spike's home of turbulence, drugs, or conventional abnormality, but I rid it of scabies and that was more than the pigeons could ever do. Before settling into the apartment, Spike, my other new housemates, RJ and Luis Deperdue, and myself had a ritualistic bonding. I made a casserole similar to the paella my grandmother would make for birthdays, holy communions, and bridal showers. Unlike my grandmother, though, we had bags of ketamine on the side. After an hour of getting to know one another, Spike was on the floor tugging at the pant legs of my pajamas yelling something about airplanes, while I enjoyed the sensation of drowning and begged for more. Luis claimed to have seen the other side. RJ repeated little offbeat noises that made us laugh, until the Misfits on the radio was all we could hear. *Welcome home.*

In my home, inhibitions—in love, sex, vices—were gone. It was okay to break down into a shambles, without feeling too inferior. It was normal

to be crazy. Nestled between sheets of lime-green alongside jet-black drywall, we didn't mind hearing one another fuck. Because while we fucked, there was a quiet resonance of rats and pigeons living in our walls. They never failed to bless our chances at a good lay. Through the windows, trucks delivering to pastry shops and lumber yards dispelled pleasant fumes. Inside, they mingled with those of tea kettles and joints to create the most humble of aromas. Our home was a palace, suffocating beneath the Brooklyn–Queens Expressway.

CHAPTER FIVE

The next step to internal redemption.

SEPTEMBER

Like manic depression, inexpensive cocaine, and life itself, it's common sense to expect coming down after coming up, whether it takes weeks, or hours. My house, collaged with mismatching upholstery and statuesque trash, was the same. Beside the headless Virgin of Guadalupe on the Corinthian column from the Bargain Bazaar was a doorway to the basement, where I slept. The visual clutter and decor in the windowless pit was equally vibrant and strategic, but also humbling. Home was like a daily psychological obstacle course, where upstairs was Los Angeles in June and downstairs was Minneapolis in February. On the opposite end of Guadalupe, wigs, thoughtful seating arrangements, pot paraphernalia, gay erotica, and large windows that almost reached the ceiling encircled a makeshift Formica kitchen. Perched beneath the Expressway overpass, home's intricacies felt permanent. That autumn, depression was just another debilitating constant I tried to comprehend.

Human existence is the engine of a 1962 Impala. It's encased in something stunning in fair weather, something beautifully cryptic when in peril, and always shifting. It can struggle on rocks and dicey terrain, but run smoothly on paved concrete with the right chemical concoction in its filters. Some humans, indefinitely, take on rocks, gravel, and foreign soil, because it makes them stronger. Some humans can make light of unwanted gravel. An engine's life expectancy depends on how well it is kept. When some engines die, they are dead. Other engines last, but they feel used, and are as good as dead. Some engines are built to last, and those are most likely maintained by rich people. But unlike the engine of an American car, America hardly hopes to preserve all rotting human hearts. And the question we now ask is, undoubtedly, how do

you fix a broken engine? In order to, of course, break it again, and be a bit better at fixing it the second time around.

Between society's quirks that torture your brain's own quirks and demons, some people are, eternally, half-broken engines of an Impala. I was crazy to think a psychological makeover could save me in a way that wouldn't create a completely new human. I could repair my brain as much as possible, but at the same time I had to accept the things I couldn't fix—an ever-changing New York, and my half-buried memories of life's earliest and darkest incidents. I sat, rusted and threatened, understanding that this was always going to be the case. And given that, I would interact only with those things that struggled with a similar turbulence, like Coney Island.

Isabelle is wild. Love can't save me, I thought one Thursday in the early morning, before I went to sleep for the day. *If it's with a man, I'll just recollect the harshest memories of the few men I've loved in my life.*

And if it's with a woman, I'll remember the part of Cuban tradition that doesn't tolerate gay love. Oops, there goes the family. I took a breath.

"Oh, I know," I said to myself, mid-panic attack, trying to enjoy a beef empanada on the paisley love seat. "I'll just take another hit off Consuela." Consuela was RJ's bong.

Empanada grease on the tips of my fingers smeared Consuela's neck, and she slipped onto the floor, shattering into several parts. *It's just one of those days*, I thought, *and this softcore porn isn't even working.* Now, finally, the time had come when I could no longer recall the euphoric instances my body knew; because it only remembered the things I had asked it to forget.

During a drug-induced moment of hypnotic therapy, I remembered a twelve-year-old me, sneering and rejecting the last visit from my father. Another memory: Stacy, an old friend, who once hawked a gentle lugie onto the crease of Randall's cheekbone while he sketched innocently into a notebook. As I returned to reality, I faced an unfortunate truth— literally spitting on the face of those who tormented me couldn't always tape to-

43

gether the fraying ends of a faltering subconscious. However, on most Thursday nights, Rhonda could.

After two hours of primping, RJ became Rhonda on the more glitzy *nights at the Palace*, which typically resulted in party hopping until the next morning. She was the wise yet reckless aunt we always wanted, who would validate our experience as young and lost. Rhonda smelled like the aunt your parents lied to you about, in order to preserve the typical humbleness of older relatives. She clouded our living room with Charlie-brand musk and a fisherman's dialect, until she had done enough cabaret shows to afford white diamonds. Rhonda carried a gold clutch, filled with first-aid lip lacquer and little bags of cocaine, to match the gold stilettos, which could last on her feet until dusk, but only if she was blown-out enough. Rhonda would shine in character and call me a "nasty cunt" in public. But I knew Rhonda would knife any bitch that tried me behind hordes of coke-snorting drunkards blocking the bathroom entrance. Rhonda was my guardian angel. In most drunken stupors, becoming her was my goal, in a perverse sense of growth.

I wanted to scout open bars, sing in public, and have drunk old men grovel at my feet. I wanted to be an old woman who still smoked pot and wore sequins in the winter. I wanted the moonlit reflections on my dress to blind whoever stood beside me hailing a cab.

On a Friday like any other, we arrive home at a staggering 8 AM.

Honey, you're a mess. Take this marijuana cigarette and have yourself a field day at the park, why don'tcha? I doubt you'll be sleeping for another day, anyway.

Yo, what the fuck?

Luis was like my brother. Not because I had known him for a very long time, but because the guy at the bodega thought we were related, and we tended to play along. Rhonda introduced me to Luis while we were on graveyard shift at the old club, Tootsie Pop. Luis appeared to be in his early twenties, but spoke in a rough antique Hollywood accent after the clock hit 3 AM. I had been weeping for days after receiving the news about Enrique's death, and Luis offered a shoulder and a bump. We grew beyond the false connections of cocaine, and ended up living together at the Palace.

CHAPTER SIX

The one-night stand I unfortunately
wished was more than a one-night stand.

OCTOBER

S*tay away from those demons who've already burned you*, my conscience told me when bidding farewell before another night out. And by demons, I knew my conscience meant cocaine. Or crank. Any happy fucking dust that pulled me through the more bitter pasts, but pushed me into even more bitter futures. Anything that kept me awake and created a numb reality. Anything with a comedown that accented emotional ambivalence; depression. Bare bones spritzed with a sense of loss—or no sense at all. When the emptiness hit me, I just did more, and came up roses.

Shut up Harvey, I told my conscience, did another rail, and left the apartment.

It was a safety mechanism. Because for a minute, after a swim through my favorite white stream, nobody mourned. For an hour, nobody had died that month. For a day, familial turmoil was negated, and the imbalances in my brain were choreographing an equilibrium as poised as ballerinas. For the night, I was sexually confident and the aftermath of abuse sat in the corner with the other puddles of spilled milk, which quickly became rancid as I became higher. There was always a way to find it for free, especially if you smelled bad and were crying, in a dress. Besides actual friends, the guys who would hook me up were otherwise chauvinistic and boring—but I felt above them, always, so I felt fine being an asshole myself, doing their drugs. Otherwise, I did what anyone would do—broke my wallet, and later pouted once it was time to pay rent. On a night like any other, I waltzed through a bar on Rivington and Ludlow or somewhere of that nature.

Truthful romantic interactions can't be found drunk, undersexed, and horny in a bar, I thought, loudly slurping a whiskey sour to the dismay of those around me. I walked into darker corners of the bar's basement, lit in a more deceitful black light. *I find my soul mates during punk rock shows and natural disasters. It's my fate.* I sat inches from a striking silhouette. *Or, am I just conditioned to think that? By, well, the Man?* I looked out of the corner of my left eye and glanced at a vision, illicit, lovely, and not yet enhanced by drunk goggles. *Fuck.*

"Carmencita Gutierrez Alonzo. My friends call me Car."

Broc Smith stuttered his words to match the whirlpool his lips made when he talked. On a night when I didn't mind the possibility of obnoxious chivalry, or a romance with a spiteful conclusion, I let Broc tell me about his life. The longer I stared, the less I saw traces of the past. The more we talked, the more I made fun of his jacket. It was a gift from his mother, so he boasted about her, in a classical method that only endeared him to me. As soon as he expressed a comfort with women who fart in public, our eyes interlaced further than our vices, and our tongues met.

In the gleam of blue lighting and overturned barstools, we made future plans. After another rail, I asked him to kiss me again. I felt the blood settle beneath my pupils and my brain stretch with a sense of wisdom, which, though false as ever, was unstoppable. Smith's tongue was inside of me, soothing the numbness between my teeth and my throat. Smith's fingers were a thrill, where I could feel his gentle massage on my shoulders trickle between my lungs and my pussy. The cocaine shifted from physical to mental and I suddenly felt a tender and submissive adoration for Smith. Flashes of a damaged past were flushed and obsolete.

However, Smith was a man, and that diverted me. The truth is, when I fucked women, I carried the phallus. I carried the silicone armor and I wielded the thoughtful size of my tiny hands. It was easy to forget why vaginal penetration had become a foreign concept to me, post-virginity. I had an overactive clitoris, gorged with a fruitful desire. It fluttered frantically and

liked it. *Who needs other organs?* I thought. *I do*, I thought again. I wanted women, Smith, and any human with their own phallus, to fuck me.

Mediocre romances kept me busy and aroused but regrettably detached from what I was supposed to be learning. Later that week, when I had forgotten what Harvey told me about cocaine, I got high with Smith. I got so high that Smith's eyes were orifices and the reflection of my body perched in them was so striking, I wanted him. I wanted him perched in my orifice. I wanted to get fucked—just not that night.

Smith was adventurous, but also like a Victorian crown molding: an ornamental treat to a smoky interior, but rigid and straightforward in quality. We could deconstruct the damaged ends of Marxism over a four-hour coke binge, but I would've had to spike his Jameson with PCP to make him enjoy all of the brightly colored doors and willow trees with me.

For now, the consequences were pleasurable. On a one-night stand followed by six tender slurps of tequila, you wake up and congratulate yourself for getting you and another person laid. After a one-night stand on rails and rails of white dust, intentions form a spiral and you feel words and hear touch. You fall in love. Every word seeps from the heart, you grab Smith's face and caress it like you're both about to die. We sought it. A quick reprieve from the tender sores of rape. For a minute, you're a visionary, a champion, blurring words in unintelligible circles that manifest into anything but the truth. They manifest as beautiful. Nose to nose, we clutched our transparent desires and trotted gleefully, hand in hand like lost kids, on a minefield that stretched for miles. But we didn't mind walking. We could do it all night.

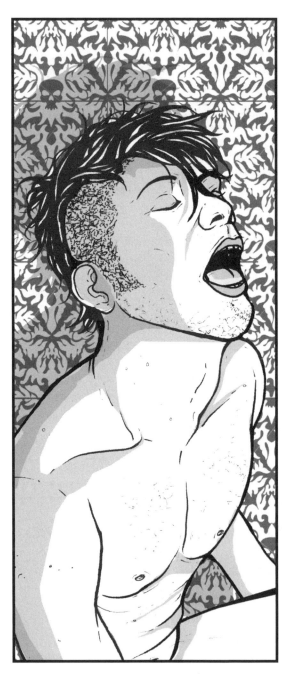

 CHAPTER SEVEN

Another shitty Friday.

C arolina waved a wing of white feathers at Marie, Leah, Luis, and myself on that New Year's Eve as the clock struck midnight. Marie and Leah were rough acquaintances of ours, but dragged us in tow to a strip club near the West Side Highway. Carolina's wings seemed heavier than asphalt but as delicate as the black curls waving back and forth from her earlobes to her cheeks and against the steel pole at the corner of the stage. Diverting one wing from her left side, Carolina smiled at us, and we smiled at the sparkling, dark, bubbly pair of tits on her chest. In a choreographed twirl, Carolina ran a wing across my face and my intuition called for resurgence. A natural high caused by the chaotic love for a stripper—Carolina of the Bronx.

After swallowing enough bourbon to make brave sentences, Luis got in a cab, the dancers put on overcoats and ordered nightcaps, and Marie and Leah introduced me to Carolina.

"Do you like girls, Carolina?" I asked.

"I love girls!"

"Can I take you out for chowder and shrimp cocktails right now?"

"Sure, but I don't date girls. I'm just saying. Before I break your heart."

"Oh, damn. Well. I like everything. We can eat chowder. Have a serious talk and break the hearts of . . . of, ugh." I lost my balance in a classic drunk shuffle, scratched my eyebrows and faced my reflection on the black tile of the sparkling floor. I regained my composure: ". . . the hearts of lonely men."

"Aw, thanks girl. But perhaps next Thursday. It's my cousin's birthday then and she's celebrating at Dick's. The fag bar. Her name is Sally. You'll like her."

"Dick's! I live with this man . . . Spike . . . He works there . . . you know.

He gets guys drunk. He's a bartender there."

"Oh, that's nice."

"Gets his balls sucked behind the counter. Ha. You know what I'm saying."

"Sure." Carolina turns and whispers to Marie. "This girl's so vulgar. I like her."

"Ugh. It was swell knowing you, Carolina. Sorry to break your heart. I have to go. I actually can't have chowder with you. I have to go."

"Honey, you need some caffeine."

"Great. I'll get some at Dick's. Bye Marie, Leah, it's been a pleasure."

I stumbled out of the door and trotted with wide steps from the West Side to the East Side, and then to Alphabet City. Evidently, I was on the 28TH day of my menstrual cycle, a time when emotional and sexual energy is all I have the desire to unleash. I walked through dilapidated little corridors that were once meatpacking factories; through aromas of grilled ribs, sawdust, and smokestacks, mingling with one another from sidewalk to sidewalk; through brick upon brick, printed beautifully with distressed advertisements for local products that saw their last run decades ago. With every step through Manhattan, I could smell the gamble, where the dice could land on preservation or destruction. *She's ever-changing, like a human.* Grasping my wallet that peeked out of the back pocket of my jeans, I looked around and hoped for a less glitzy future. Change was beautiful, I thought, but puritanical success wasn't made for the devil's playground. Carolina was endangered like gay bars, like people of color. However, she, like her counterparts, wouldn't sleep to the song of surrender.

We aren't going anywhere, I think to myself, crossing Avenue A, thirty feet from Dick's. *What are you gonna do, man? Make the people illegal too?* Visions of the deportation of anyone not an upper-crust, card-carrying consumer rush

me, unwelcomed. *Well, only a couple streets are crushed. I put on blinders to make my insides feel good. The local vendors and shops, and the freak contingent at the opening night of* A Chorus Line? *They just, you know—moved away. And all those gay bars that closed down? They just went "poof" one day. But they'll be back.* And I walked toward the door of Dick's.

"New York's like, my voodoo doll, baby," I said, propping myself on a stool to reach eye level with Myrtle Willoughby, a black-haired queen in red pumps.

"Oh really?" Myrtle was interested.

"Yeah, when she gets a fucking slice of integrity, I get a fucking broken heart. Shit hits the fan. Some shit gets between my toes and I can hardly make it across the fucking living room."

"Depression is a bitch, girl."

"It's less of a bitch when I have that other bitch, snow white."

"Oh girl, me and snow white severed ties on my 30TH birthday."

"Hell knows if our relationship will last that long." My eyes wandered as I tried to keep my balance.

"You know, when New York dies, we're all gonna party so fucking hard in hell."

"Fuck New York dying. I'm going out with more forthcoming blows. Coney Island, I guess."

"So when Coney Island is destroyed, you're going to hell?" Myrtle asks.

"Fuck yeah. I can smell it. I can smell the fucking grilled ribs and smoke rings. No one else can. See, I've got this psychic, her name is—damn."

"What?"

"Look at her."

"That's Sally. It's her birthday."

As I stared, a glistening mass of woman waltzed through the door. It was Rhonda. Like a proud mother boasting about her roasted bird on Thanksgiving Day, Rhonda was showing off her new mink. I could only dream of owning such self-assurance. I sunk in dishonor.

"Honey, I brought you poppers!" she yelled.

Rhonda waved a little brown bottle with the word "Rush" inscribed on a yellow label. She whispered into my ear: "It makes you, you know, loose. Embracing anything big, and you know, hard. Get it? Just inhale."

Rhonda was a redeemer, but also an enabler who repeatedly lit the fuse. I was a helpless firecracker.

"Oooh. Nice. Thanks Mom," I said.

Rhonda put me to shame, but I never told her so. I felt more confident as a simpler woman. But confidence seemed so easy if you were six feet tall and wore MAC makeup nightly. Confidence seemed fast approaching if you sang like Liza Minnelli on purple nightclub stages after smoking acres of marijuana. She made happiness seem feasible.

"Rhonda, you make happiness seem feasible."

"Oh honey, I'm just blown out." Rhonda was humble.

"Oh, that reminds me." I reached for a telephone to call Smith so I could have sex later that night and, possibly, fall in love. I walked into a quiet corner where a string of red Christmas lights adorned a framed photograph of Freddy Mercury, which made the bricks resemble burning coal. I squatted on the ground and listened to a vibrant moaning, emitting from the crack beneath a door that read EMPLOYEES ONLY.

"I love poppers!" yelled a man who was probably getting fucked very well for the first time. "I love you!" yelled another man, who was either on copious amounts of co- caine, or he had achieved what I thought was impossible this day and age. He was actually in love. As I began to dial, I tumbled hap- lessly into a deep longing for blow. I always felt embarrassed over my low tolerance for any drug. I could watch Spike, Rhonda, Smith, Luis, and whoever the fuck blow nightly rails and never seem to want to die after the week is over—just sleep. A lot. And because I was relative- ly scared of dying, I would stop snorting for the night as soon as my heart was running faster than my brain. However, the routine was always a bust—because af- ter thirty hours, the excitability wanes, the walls begin to look gray, and I soon want to die again. And then, consequently, begins anoth- er night of riding bareback on the white horse.

Slouching on the carpet, a desire to construct happiness enveloped me: I'd forgotten that true love exists (somewhere, with whomever, and whatever caliber of love it may be) while I sat here, nose burning in surrender. A rage entangled me as the moans grew louder and louder. The men sounded joyous, and I perched myself on the carpet like a sour voyeur without anything better to do. Placing my fists on my chin, I looked down and closed my eyes. Thoughts were sickening, and my brain vegetated in a state of unrest. I didn't picture these possibly sexy, pleasant employees enjoying one another's company. I only thought of Randall.

Randall never would have gone to jail if I told the police what he had done to me through sex and love. Manipulation isn't illegal. Randall wasn't illegal, the way so many people in New York City were. Society has always been bad at deciding wrong from right. Because, according to the law, I'm just some bipolar junky who happened to have been sexually assaulted once or twice, and later mind-fucked by some crass romantic I shouldn't have trusted anyway. Perhaps I'm just pulling the abuse card in order to justify my irresponsible lifestyle. *Blah, blah.* I knew society was wrong anyway. You know something's wrong when Manhattan's finest need more proof of harm to act on domestic violence than to arrest someone for smoking a joint.

I couldn't afford a lawyer even if such laws on manipulation existed in America. Randall maneuvered his smile through the cracks in my confidence and eased his own conscience through aloofness and little forged *I'm Sorry*s. In the past, trying to provide support to—and receiving it from—people who had been in violent relationships made this healing process much easier for me.

"But a scar is a scar," I thought out loud. I rubbed my eyes, trying to wipe away memory, the way I rubbed my eyes to wake from an out-of-body experience after taking too big a hit off the now-deceased Consuela. The little bottle of poppers rolled from my pocket to the carpet and landed, label up. "Rush," it said, telling my body tastefully to move on with a kindhearted

70

spirit. *Poppers aren't false, like cocaine. And men like Randall will never be illegal the way poppers are. Come here, darling.*

The door opened and bodies tumbled like laundry onto the carpeted hallway where I conversed with myself. *How many people are having orgasms right now?* I thought. For a second, running into the stalls to rub one out seemed perfectly appropriate. I pressed my ear against the carpet to feel the vibration of a Pretenders song that played in the main lounge.

"Girl. That was outrageous. I see you're next?" Spike perched himself next to me after waltzing out of the storage room rosy-cheeked and dry.

"No I'm just holding these poppers, thinking about if I'll ever want to kiss someone without anything in my nostrils. You know, the usual self-deprecation," I told Spike, and he held me closely.

Our sweat intermingled, mine reeking of pesto and oil, his of sexual misconduct. We smiled at one another, then at the little bottle of poppers, as if it were a little child of our own. Spike took a whiff and laughed.

CHAPTER EIGHT

Make me bleed somewhere else next time,
if there is a next time.

P oppers. Porn shop patrons and sales clerks refer to them as "liquid incense," "VCR head cleaner," or any scientific jargon to allow the legal sale of a substance designed to shoot our blood vessels into the stars for a moment of serenity. They provide us with a three-minute orgasm and are safer than mixing aspirin with a top-shelf cocktail. When you're tired, you stop. When your head aches, you lie around and drink eight ounces of water. The chance of fainting is nearly impossible. With tiny bottles, you don't lose inhibitions, only inabilities. Poppers are one of the most pleasurable concoctions the world has ever seen. But in America, pleasure seems to be either banned or frowned upon—and it makes us all lost, sexually deviant junkies.

That night at 3 AM, when I had the poppers in me, I said hello to Sally. She had perfect pink tresses draping her cheeks, making her look like a boyish hell-raiser in a leather miniskirt. Sally had a cute "girl power" insignia latched onto her tattered cotton t-shirt, only mere inches from the deadly piranha encircling the side of her neck. Her fair skin bore freckles all over and her half-smile said trouble in bold lettering, engraved in toxic sign-painter's enamel.

"Hey, I'm Sally. I just moved here from Berlin. Do you know where I can meet girls?"

"I'm a girl. I just moved here from Florida. That's not that cool, but you know, whatever, I'm over it. Are you?"

Sally smiled and stood several inches closer, so the heat from her skin tickled the hairs on my arms. Sally was like a slab of slick wool. I felt utter guilt feeling her skin on mine. Harvey, my conscience, reminded me that night of all the butchered souls that had to lie dead or with a swollen heart in order for me to enjoy her flirting.

"I like that," I said, pointing at the piranha. My fingers felt that poison puritans would often condemn as adultery. Sally stared at me, and I stared back without a cocaine crutch or any unfair comparisons to the old flames that burned me.

We kissed on the leather sofas of Dick's, disregarded the dry cum stains, scoffed at the one gazing straight guy, and watched my friends leave without me. What would, in most cases, have been a crash-and-burn fling in the corner of the room resulted in an unconditional attraction. Sally pulled me from the waistline to mumble something about her apartment in the West Village into my beer-soaked ear.

"Do you want to go to my apartment in the West Village?" she asked while two men paraded around us yelling some jargon about everyone being in love. "I'm a painter. I'll show you my oil paintings."

"That sounds lovely. I hate oil painting. I'm terrible at it. I like it when people aren't terrible at it. It makes me want to see what their hands have that mine don't."

"I'll show you what my hands can do. I'll show you my teeth too."

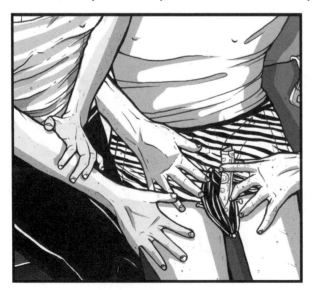

"Your teeth," I kindly mocked her.

We hopped in a cab outside of Dick's and rode down to Hudson on the West Side. We arrived, and Sally reached into her wallet to pay the complete fare. I wasn't used to chivalry.

*   *   *

78

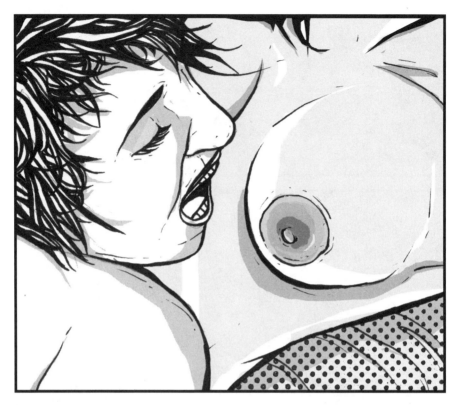

Sally's apartment was like an antique shop in the Village, after its foreclosure by the city. The clutter was charming. We pranced through her leather chests, unveiled a little box of pornography, put it on the television, and danced on her upholstery. We fucked on a barstool and a couch with dozens of torn seams. Sally put her hands in me and all I heard was music. Outside the window, a jazz quartet performed a morning serenade to please the kids who had been up all night. That was us, with vigor that existed only from attraction, her German accent, my Latin curves, and strings of words existing without blow.

"Darling, I love your cunt," Sally told me, and I smiled. I remembered we were all okay. I almost came, but Sally let go of my clitoris, crept up towards my chest, and our eyes interlaced.

I walked to the train with the illicit vision of Sally's beautiful face. My last nerve burst inexplicably, and tears flooded my eye sockets. Soon, I felt my arms again and the drunkenness, the poppers, and the night faded. I could smell a manic interval shattering through shitty experience after shitty experience. I looked up at the dreary lining of every New York cloud clashing with nature. It began to rain and I tried to wipe away the blood seeping through the fabric of my shirt.

Do the unhappy endings of affairs prove the puritan theories behind the anti-pleasure agenda? Or maybe they prove we are imperfect humans with imperfect affairs that resort to puritanical theories for self-protection? Damn. Are imperfections finally making me stronger? In my drunken stupor, I continued this train of thought. *Hopefully this is what will come of this. Almost losing my nipple in combat, and all.* I looked back at the spark of our bodies pressed against one another. An awkward morning is always better than a boring night, I thought. But these little thoughtless tangents kept killing the moment. Wanting cocaine. Smith. Tatiana. The blood on my left tit. I caught the train home, keeping my face down, surrendering to the permanent stains on my favorite t-shirt. Happy fucking new year.

I arrived at my room around 8 AM and received a message from Tatiana. She lived in Florida and I had lusted after her for years. Our affair took its toll, but my false hope still ran wild. Tatiana was a devilish lover who bled through the cracks of every affair that followed. The morning after the nights we had sex, we hardly spoke of what had happened, but we knew the glare of our teeth burned one another's eyes from smiling. Tatiana was ambidextrous, half-Mexican, and from the South. She rejected my plea to be a pair, but I hid the hurt to facilitate the fond farewell that took place minutes before hopping in a U-Haul that smelled like a basement and headed to New York City.

"Yeah girl! I'm at the bridge! I just pissed and it hit a fucking pigeon! The sun is about to rise and I'm fucking sprung from eight shots of Jack!

Yeah! So like, you are the memories that last even when my brain is fucking fried. I miss you, bitch." I settled my enthusiasm into that terrible niche of false hope, adorning my thoughts with weak theory.

"Tatiana isn't my fucking father. She'll come the fuck back," I told myself.

CHAPTER NINE

Intermission in the third dimension.

I tended to use my money rashly. Whenever I found myself both broke and depressed, I just smoked acres of weed for a psychological fix and rummaged around a slew of dealers for the occasional psychiatric drug binge. I didn't want a daily fix—just a little minute where I could skew the moments that otherwise kill me.

Like a rainstorm at the end of an overcast weekend, my depression burst into feeling that night on the F train while leaving Sally's apartment. I was tired of chemical splurges redirecting my traumas and terrible trains of thought. I wanted to crawl into my skull and retrieve a saving grace, without the aid of lines and lovers, to kill the couple of months when depression owned me. This was a goal I had for years and finally grasped, clenched tight—figuring out what my body needs when nothing means anything and all it sees are scars.

Mental health is a series of realizations for me. First, I grin at my reflection and realize I can do most of the things I've forever wanted to do. Then, I remember why I do such things. Soon, passion and balance tug at one another, and rest content at my bedside and in my innards. The manic era that follows most descents into self-loathing reminds me that for the most part, we are all okay. I hold onto this intensity for dear life. I don't want pills to suppress my own biological chemistry, and just to dull self-loathing. This was why Harvey insisted on hiding the coke, and I insisted that all prescription drugs were too anesthetizing.

So, I sought an understanding voice of reason when the dark ages would come again. *I can't afford that psychotherapist, but fuck it, I'll think about this later*, I thought to myself one morning. Because at the time, I was manic.

It was the dead of winter in the Palace under the expressway. Mania woke me beside teetering rats and half-dead pigeons that rolled gleefully inside the drywall of my damp little basement bedroom. After one morning of recapturing my self-worth, I stopped needing the blow, the blowjobs, and the occasional violent daydreams involving blows to the skull.

I walked outside to shovel the sidewalk while Carlos and Diego, the owners of the bodega on the corner, smiled at me. We chatted and I felt a fondness for everything I knew growing up in Miami. The daily routine was this: wake by the sunlight, prance barefoot on eighty-degree concrete, and yap nonsense in Spanish to hordes of people.

The loveliness of this reminded me to make a list on notebook paper of everything I hated. Everything that ruined me and everything I abandoned for the last couple of years because it was too perplexing to face. I folded the sheet of paper, kissed it goodnight, and slipped it into my safe.

I'll deal with your bullshit later. I have to go be manic right now. Enjoy life while I can, you know? But I swear to you, baggage, I'm not moving out like I've

done since I was seventeen. New York and I are an irrepressible duo. I'm gonna grind you between my teeth and make the best of you in order to make the best of me. But for now, I have to go on vacation and do drugs. I truly apologize for the irresponsibility that comes with thinking life is fucked. Later assholes.

*   *   *

I walked toward Spike's bedroom door and remembered which loose bolt was so difficult to fix—that one that was suppressing the worth in anything. I walked further and re-membered how to quell skepticism and scavenge for that worth because I'm so sure it's there, in my veins and in my nerves. And that felt good. I grabbed Spike's doorknob and remembered that that's progress. I walked into a hangover, jumped on his velvet upholstery, and made plans for a celebration.

"Let's go get tanked in Florida! Cheap flights and sunshine that burns our souls with nature's tox-ins!" I put on a calming serenade of Los Crudos on his record player and straddled his weeping body. "Oh please Spike! Let's go to Florida!"

"Okay sure dude . . . yeah totally." Spike rolled over, drooling on the sheets, assuring me of his word. Spike was nearly human, but constructed like a temple of divine authority, obviously cherished by flocks of scantily clad Greek men, and which provided the absolute truths Plato, Xenophon, and Herodotus sought after. Spike abided by the laws of the ocean, and only the laws of the ocean. Somewhere between a Manhattan bartender and the scum of the earth, Spike was wise beyond his years and he painstakingly criticized society's expectations of love and survival. He judged the potential of his lovers on their knowledge of Iron Maiden, as opposed to parenting skills or kindness.

I met Spike traveling through New England, when we were still unsure of how to survive alongside our opposition. As a lost tween, Spike fled to punk rock when Christianity bit him on the ass. As a lovely twenty-some-thing, Spike fled to New York City when straight-laced heterosexuality bit him on the groin. Spike and I created a rough and tumble dynamic that justified the brilliance most self-proclaimed head-bangers often forgot to claim. Spike was the only one of my friends who would dance with me to '90s rock when we were high as kites and attempting to obliterate the trepidation of an overwhelming week of work, or jail. That February, we broke from the cold and flew to Florida on what was possibly the first weekend of the year that cultivated any high spirits whatsoever. We chose my birthplace for retreat on some sick impromptu measures, and there we were, smearing sunscreen on the skin above our palpitating hearts.

*   *   *

After arriving at Miami International Airport, we made our way to the coast, where I heard illegal hijinks might still circulate. Spike and I shuffled alongside pot dealers on the Ocean Drive strip, and pretended the newly constructed, heinous glass structures were actually glaring, colored temples. Miami was the same landmine as New York, except with more strip malls.

While revisiting tragic antique holes along Collins, I came to learn my favorite family-run Argentine bakery had gone to the chains. The lost kids

who typically foraged on the strip retreated further north for cheaper pizza, though they risked the possible abomination of undercover narcs.

South Beach was steadily growing according to the tastes of the rich and famous, but still seeking an immigrant benediction. South Beach was not supposed to be this white.

The sun set like a time bomb as we set aside our complaints, because there wasn't really anything I could do about the destruction right then and there. After all, I wasn't half as suicidal as I had been recently, as a burnt-out, terribly lost, human rights activist. If I were ever to erect another pillar against patriarchy or smash another state, I would need rejuvenation. Humans are designed so that they can only properly save the world after having first saved themselves. So for serenity's sake, we partied like we would in hell that weekend.

*   *   *

Sleek deco patios—decorated with clean imported seagulls—paved the tourist strip that I used to call home. Spike and I had pinned down three winter days on our calendar reserved for nothing but recovering from our brains and jobs. We arrived in Miami to uncomfortable glares from passersby, and architecture so manicured, that the manic retreat had its slight imperfections. As opposed to rotting, our 'pit stains were sparkling, as we blew paychecks like dicks on a Friday night after a week of fasting and celibacy. We walked on the strip en route to our motel.

"You guys are rock 'n' rollers aren't you? Are you from London?" a middle-aged American couple sipping mojitos asked us, voyeurs of the Latin flair, gawking to our dismay.

I swiped my finger against a steel pole and felt a heat unlike any steel pole in wintry old New York. At dusk, we settled into our motel and met with several relocated New Yorkers. They fed us chivalry and ecstasy. Spike played in the shower and I swung off the railing of a little iron balcony. Everybody inside the room was rolling, but MDMA hardly worked for me. I heard it was once used as an anxiety medication, which explained my uncontrollable desire to pack envelopes and alphabetize the items in the kitchen.

The smiles around the room enchanted me. For a minute, I remembered why we did the things we did: our responsible passions kept us ticking. Everyone inside worked to pay the bills and lived to feed the soul. On the side they created music, picked up telephones, bartended to hungry people, and talked to strangers like myself. Friendships had blossomed by virtue of a little nick in psychiatric medicine in Florida's sun-stricken confines.

But the city grew dull, the beach blankets crowded by debris and a resurrection of tourists, and I forgot this was ever my humble terrain. Our New York friends left our side, and Spike and I downed a bottle of champagne and waltzed through town in search of something that would transform reality into a carnival. During high school, when I was in detention hall, waiting to skip prom to go to a punk rock show in South Beach, the rest of the kids I knew roved South Beach in search of hits of acid and other atypical Miami hallucinogens. I may be manic, but I was still on a soul search. The possibility of finding myself by getting too drunk off champagne was nearly impossible. On that night, I wanted the acid that I had missed out on in high school so bad. Because if any vice is going to properly assist any soul-searching, it's acid. And if acid's potent anywhere outside of San Francisco, it's Miami Beach.

"Dude, I'm tripping balls." A young guy fell beside us as we exited a café.

"Where did you get it?" Spike inquired and my anxiety waned, as I felt closer to the next realm.

"That raver guy over there. Dude. What?"

I remember those sixteen hours when we couldn't stop the laughter; everything was dripping with a blue and green hysteria. Feelings had color and wind tasted the way it smelled. The lining on each Florida cloud touched the phosphorescence in the distance, on the Atlantic Ocean. Flashes of light illuminated our faces; and as soon as time ceased to exist, it was Spike and me versus the world. Blessed delirium hit us on Collins where we met up with friends at some straight shoe-gazer party where even the rowdies were stale and dry. Spike started swinging on a pole and I jumped beside him and bent backwards in a fierce rendition of drunken yoga.

"That isn't allowed here, the pole is for girls only." We stared with our dilated pupils.

"What? What kind of chauvinist dive is this?"

"It's the rules, Miss."

"Honey, we have to get out of here."

Broken conventions, vio-
lations, and disarray followed
us no matter where we went.
A little down the street was a
lesser-known gay bar with no
cover and specials on something pink, cheap, and delicate.
The dancer poles were made of
ice and sprouted from wooden
planks in a bar that looked like
a pirate ship. We danced around
the oxygen streaming onto the
dance floor from the bamboo
shades, which were slowly turning the color of our dirty palms
that blended smoothly with the
grit of my city. We clenched
the poles and swung around.
I was serious about movement;
I learned it kept me alive.

"Honey, the pole is for guys
only."

"What?"

"The pole, it's for guys
only."

"I AM THE POLE," I whis-
pered into the bartender's ear,
as two lanky boys in Guayabera
shirts, sipping lush tropical
cocktails, approached me.

"Who is your friend? Oh my god can we fuck him? Don't be a cock-blocking fag-hag!" they squealed and I wanted to say they were just not Spike's type. I wanted to say to quit believing that he'd bone them, even if they were the last boys on earth. I wanted to say get away from us—*this is a journey of the soul, not the genitalia.* I wanted to spurt out an unparalleled wisdom that would make them question their tactless approach to getting fucked forever and always, so they would never impose their bodies on a body that doesn't want it.

"No bitches, we're tripping on fucking acid," I smiled and peered over in Spike's direction as he waltzed to our corner. He was bored, inattentive, and over the boys. That night was for us alone—we existed as wolves in an uncharted landscape being unfortunately catapulted into a civil future. We were here to save Miami and to save ourselves. The ends of the earth were near, but the two boys insisted on an unpleasant chase, as we ran east to watch the fluorescent strip shrink and the ocean sprawl naked before us.

Eventually, we reached the end of the earth. The horizon was jeweled and the ocean wrapped itself in a coil of static lines and shadows shaped like dancing people. We dropped all baggage and sighed at the sight of the Atlantic on the country's southern tip.

"Fuck! Those fucking kids stole my wallet! But wait, look. It looks like there's something between that giant cube of water and the sand." Spike marveled at the paradox by which chemical beauties were, for sixteen hours, enough to conceal our bullshit. Distressed, identities stolen, and shirts half-torn, we smiled. We walked from the ocean towards the motel.

"New York is alright, man," I told Spike, as the eyes of passersby swelled.

"If Rhonda was here, she would make her dead fox stole come to life."

"If . . . well . . . I'm not making much sense anymore. I want to open and close an umbrella."

"Well, look, there are people standing on every rooftop. Woah," Spike confessed.

"That is really great, man." I applauded his treasure. We reached the motel to discover the lock had been jacked. As all tenants awaited a rescue by the rear exit, we came to learn none of us spoke the same language. Austria was indecisive and had bad telephone reception, Brazil was a bunch of self-contained lovers, Indonesia was on pills and ecstasy, and humble old New York sat pale-faced in the corner. Scratching ourselves, as our heads and arms began inflating and deflating, we eventually went in, to a mess of clouds and singing whistles that I recalled being furniture earlier that day.

"Hey pretty lady, you want to hang out?" I looked up at the orange canvas cover and white plastic stretches of an oversized umbrella on the balcony. "Your threads are ecstatic. Orange. The color of fury."

"Um. Car. That's not a girl. It's a totem pole," Spike said with concern.

"A totem pole that holds the earth's inconspicuous reasons for torturing humankind with unyieldingly complex emotions." I redirected my focus on the umbrella.

"Honorable one. Let down your silken arches of wisdom and caress me with knowledge—what is my purpose?" I closed the umbrella as the orange canvas encircled my body.

"The men on the horizon are going to kill us all. The other end of the platform of this fine city is creating the sickest landscape." Spike developed his own anger. "I've never—NEVER—seen a city as filthy as this. Car? Can you hear me?"

"No. I'm being fucked by this umbrella."

"No you're not, you just got stuck inside of it. Here, let me get you out."

"Well, let's go listen to music, I'm bored already." We ran back into the hotel room as inanimate objects began flying and Lynyrd Skynard's "Freebird" played on a tiny, lo-fi radio.

*　　*　　*

I had fortunately convinced myself that if I didn't stop throwing objects like cereal boxes, glasses of water, friends, and umbrellas, I would vomit. For a minute I sat cross-legged on the balcony, and to the sounds of car horns, commotion enveloped me, and my path darkened. So I did it. I vomited as verbal and physical forward progress came to an unfortunate halt. It was like

attesting to a mystical theory that existed for my twenty-five years on this earth—do or die. Or in this case, do or vomit. I felt more womanly than I ever had.

"Do you get this, man?"

"No. You vomited when you sat down. This is nonsense. And why am I pink? I am a PINK PERSON."

"Really man. This is like . . . my purpose. This is the explanation of my existence. A message from the acid gods saying to continue the fight against the bullshit I typically piss on."

"What is?"

"To THROW SHIT. And if I stop—I puke. And I don't like to do that."

Throwing shit. We defined throwing shit as "overthrowing double standards that persist as blockades to keep us from moving forward." We chose to throw shit. Ten hours later, as colors became less vivid and language less incoherent, an insect avalanche maneuvering its way through our skin was one of the last remaining sensory reminders of our journey through time and space. We arrived at the airport, frowned at the truth that all food still tasted heinous, and rode home in an airplane.

"Darling, it's our song," I said.

A videotaped concert performance of "Freebird" was playing on the airplane televisions.

"These are the moments I wish we were on the plane instead of in it."

"Totally."

CHAPTER TEN

Mother wore sequins
and the children wore black.

F or two weeks, I felt filthier and more exhausted than I had in years. The hallucinogenic sensation of insects on my skin remained with me for several days after returning home. After a twenty-four hour disco nap, all tenants of the Palace were high on life. Through the hole in the ceiling of our building, a gust of spring tapped our shoulders. *Carry on, scum of the earth*, said spring with a pleasant blow that felt nice for a second. Still feeling manic, I took a minute—which lasted a week—to appreciate what I had. In a static wrinkle between our front door and the entrance to the L train, I felt free. Fucked up, but free. That night, Manhattan lent itself to us.

"We're all doing so good tonight," Rhonda boasted, as we caroused like headless chickens on a twilight subway ride to 1st Avenue. "Tonight is going to be good, I know it. We are all looking great. We all look great in our cropped jackets. So great."

"Oh, and me without my anal douche," Luis obliged.

We entered Manhattan and exited the subway car to a night less cold than those winter typically regurgitated on us. We were just imperfect people living imperfect lives, but for some reason, we felt really damn gorgeous that evening. Walking along 1st Avenue, we headed to Dust, the weekly party Spike threw, where outrageous hordes of freaks, queers, sluts, and delinquents coalesced beneath sputtering Day-Glo and sequined wallpaper. Heads thrashed to punk rock and late '70s progressive rock as adulthood carried the same sense of aimless rebellion adolescence did.

Returning to my spot at the bar, I watched queens do girls' nails and two awkward, former lays wait in line for the bathroom. Luis stood in line with friends and gazed at me, wide-eyed. When I met Luis, I thought he was a millionaire because he went home to some place in Chelsea every night. Eventually I learned he was only a pissed-off kid who lived with his parents in a neighborhood on the West Side that had gone from the occasional refuge for the gay and distressed to the occasional bistro for the rich and repressed. His story was better than the lavish lifestyle I'd imagined, and a friendship ensued beyond the boundaries of nightlife. We reminisced as we entered the bathroom for a fix.

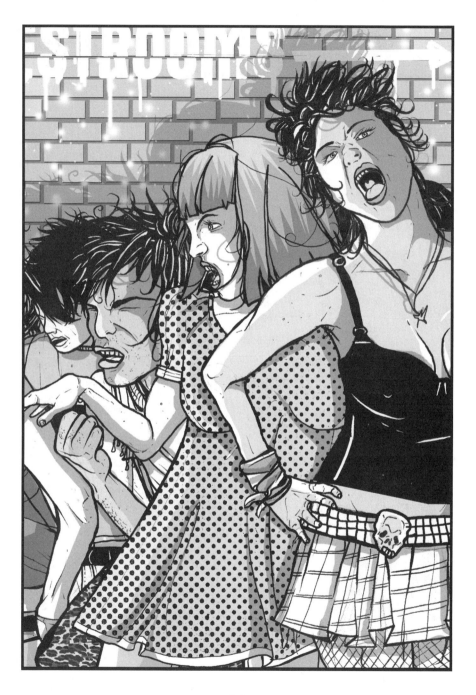

"They were the best of times, they were the worst of times," Luis recited. "To cocaine." I mocked our lifestyle in a faux mid-Atlantic accent. Luis and I exited the bathroom and Spike began to spin Nirvana.

* * *

For most of my life, I sought outrageous variety, where stank armpits could contrast kindly with a pair of stilettos and a full face. As alternative teenagers become alternative adults, their wayward upbringing either supports them through identity transitions or kills their self-assurance. I'd begun to realize punk rock wasn't always female, let alone gay. And gay nightlife was never gritty enough, and often too binary. But at Dust I felt an inner balance. Refusing to choose between male or female, punk rock or not, the queer, rock 'n' roll Dust was the brilliant offspring of Spike, Rhonda, and our friend Wella. We all needed jobs, so Spike and Wella worked as DJs at Dust, and Rhonda hosted each gala in a beautiful gown. They spun old punk records, the occasional Caribbean obscurity, Iron Maiden, and some dance remixes.

A disco ball, duct-taped to the ceiling, encircled me with incandescent spots. Nirvana was inside of me, streaming through my blood like an electric pulse of shock rehabilitation. And while I knew it wasn't real, suppose it *was* real? You have to accept any chemically altered state of mind as a legitimate human feeling.

A stranger's arms lifted me above the glass tiles, and I tumbled over heads, wigs, hats, and appendages. I knew every word to the fucking song, and I wanted everyone to know that. Aggressively mimicking every drum fill with my fists, I felt the spark of euphoria that is eventually killed by a harsh loathing once it's over.

It was difficult to believe that my ability to love my life, in a sea of disaster, for that one night was not felt by my own soul, but rather was the cause of some drug. I'd unveiled mysterious nicks in my life and I'd made plans to change while on all classes of drugs. Some chewed up my integrity near

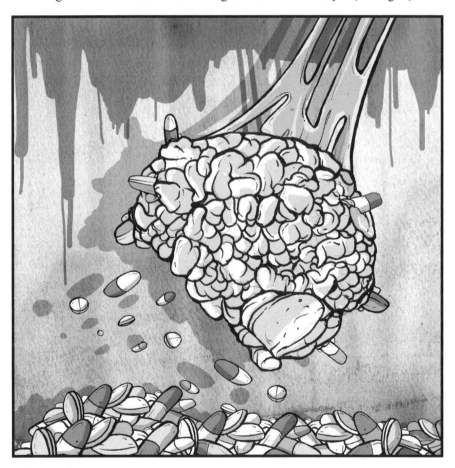

the end, rendering me a complete prototype for what they tell kids they'll become if they fuck up. Some gave me several hours of dissecting the matter my brain was truly composed of—every scar, every yellow ribbon. Some were just a fun time with friends beneath willow trees and pleasant weather. I threw out the possibility that I was just coked. I wanted this uncontrollable joy to be a sign that I'd believe in love again.

I won't let this shit burn me, I told myself, keying a bump up my right nostril. Our sentiments were truthful, I thought, whether they lasted ten minutes or were a daily fix, prescribed by a doctor or by oneself. Denying any destructive side effect, I ran outside into the crowd. We were a pill generation; pills for every imperfection. I didn't want to be a product of such a generation. Pills can bolster you if it's entirely necessary. But believing in pills didn't mean I needed to suppress all of my internal malfunctions. And while at times I found myself needing chemical rehabilitation, I wanted another way to stay alive.

Dust was real, and Dust was legal—astonishing, I thought. Dust was the first place where I could rub shoulders with people from my several walks of life. For a minute, at Dust, people who had almost nothing in common were

in this together. Such hopefulness may have been sickening, for the truth testified that not all young rebels would, or will, get along. The straightedge kids will continue to pin the drunkards to the wall, ignoring the fact that they may both hate the rest of the world according to very similar terms. The broke kids will have every right to scoff at the rich kids, while the rich kids may have their own epilogue of pain. And in the end, even our alternative world is imperfect in a myriad of understandable ways. But on a Thursday night at Dust, we dodged the bullshit and held one another in mid-dance, content, despairing, intoxicated, sober—but mostly intoxicated.

We could hardly hear one another speak, so we learned the value of body language. We hardly knew one another's names until someone called the shots on the next clean tea party—there, we learned names and processed our feelings and remembered for a second that life outside of Dust deserved a harsh cleansing. However, mastering the art of getting over your bullshit could only happen through shameless revelry on an evening at Dust. To our hearts' contentment, Spike offered Jägermeister shots to Wella and me, and we drank while I complained about someone's loose hands during my time in flight. Until destructiveness tapered, we entered a temporary stage of life where we really only wanted Jäger. We obliged and drank "to tonight."

Pleasure, in the eyes of those at Dust, was okay. It didn't matter that I had suffered the night before. What mattered was not what we were often deemed to be, but what we aspired to be in that year, or on that night. It didn't even matter that I saw Sally pacing through the bathroom corridor without even saying *hi*. Yes, for a minute my stomach sank despairingly, imagining how it might feel for Sally to be my girlfriend. But the song ended and I remembered her smile and the way she begged for mystery and how I loved this and how a successful one night stand could reign in a splendor I chose to embrace until I secretly fell in love. Love was tossed between the sluts and the drunks, but the filthy heads on the margins found some rendition of love quite often—with a sole partner or seventeen of them.

Maybe I'll soon find that elusive combination of clitoral erections and emotional investment, I thought, *but for now I'm in this crowded room, and I just want ass.*

Walking through rows of people, the cocaine settled in my cranial attic. I went from thinking everyone adored me to thinking everyone loathed me. For a minute, I missed the comfort of any setting but this New York City nightlife. The sexy, intoxicating laughs exiting everyone's glossy lips went from sounding like "I love you" to "Fuck you" to "Fuck me" as my steps widened and I reached the opposite end of the bar.

"Oh my god, you're fucking gorgeous!" some man in a feather boa and six-inch heels caressed in puff paint said to me, when I got tired of walking. I smiled and we drank to yet another revelation.

From the corner of my eye, I saw Smith at the bar. He smiled in my direction and one sexy, chancy smirk led to another. The evening ran dry and eventually we were on my bedroom floor.

* * *

I assumed Smith had an astounding little life outside of our scandalous, precious box. I was sure I had seen it through the falsehood, flowing pitifully through the veins on his arms. Blood vessels peeped through his eyeballs and his unsettling hands seemed to cater to a life I could possibly adore. Smith was full of facts and whirlwind aspirations that

danced blindly between philosopher, rock star, and outlaw. Brilliance exited Smith's mouth, as my mouth assured him of his intelligence, though we knew cracked teeth and a vibrating smile were the default expressions of people on cocaine.

"So have you gotten it up the ass?" I asked Smith as he rolled a cigarette.

"No, but we should try. We have to start small though."

"That is really great. I'm used to having a silicone penis. Fucking people's holes is a substantial part of my bisexual identity, you know."

"Oh, I never thought of it that way."

"I feel very balanced when I fuck dudes in the butt, don't you know what I mean? For the last two years I've mostly fucked girls. And I mean that literally. I happen to like boys too—my groin just can't change its interests for them."

"Yeah, yeah, that makes all the sense in the world!"

"I know."

"So why has it been so long? Can I ask?"

"Shitty ex-boyfriends. I don't want to talk about it right now."

CHAPTER ELEVEN

The last straw always drops
on a barstool at 2 AM.

MARCH

I woke up on my twin-size mattress, hardly remembering either the nourishment or toxicity of the last seven hours. Smith was naked, next to me, and I held him tenderly, as if he were the last lover I would ever experience. Forcing its way through my body was a physical zeal I had not felt in years. Unexplainable, I thought. Was I falling for Smith? Had I experienced the first fruitful fuck with a man in ages? The morning ended at 3 PM.

"When we fuck, we talk. Before, after, and during," I told Luis, during an afternoon in what I called the parlor, but was clearly a dilapidated concrete dugout behind the basement door.

"Isn't that how it's supposed to be?"

"Supposed to. It's outrageous. We don't only talk about the sex though. We talk about our lives."

"Oh. Watch out, he's a bit, I don't know. I heard he's in love with some girl."

"Oh. Yeah, another girl he fucks. I fuck other people too, you know. I fucked Sally."

"Until she made your tits bleed and you cried like a baby all the way home. Ha."

"Oh Luis, you nasty cunt."

"You miss Sally now, don't you? Don't you wish you didn't care about your tits bleeding?"

"Totally. I blame blow. Whatever. I can't be in love now anyway."

"What if you were? By mistake?"

"Impossible. Smith bores me. You know, when we aren't fucking. Or slurping our own two straws."

"With your nostrils."

"Sure."

"Sure darling." Luis left the room and I hung my head low in embarrassed defeat.

*   *   *

I attempted love with Smith, but our striking differences and the amount of cocaine stuffed in our nostrils at the moments when our lips met always seemed like evidence enough for me never to fall in love with him. And while Smith was falling in love with another woman, my feelings swung from complacency to jealousy. I was well aware the damage was done the moment Smith cuffed my wrists against the pipes on my ceiling, licking and swallowing his way to my heart. I was well aware, while Smith boasted of the texture of my skin as it coiled its way through his tattooed loins, while all I could hear was a heartbeat darting at the pace of a blown-out cheetah under fire. However, reciprocity was unlikely. Later that evening, after nightcaps at Dick's, I was offered a rail, said yes, and deliciously smeared it along my gums, my nostrils, and my defenses.

"I hate Smith, I really do. That stupid bitch was using me for sex and I hate him. He can have all the sincerity in the world with some ho bag, see if I care."

I did another rail and faced Luis, Spike, and Rhonda in a despairing squalor; my lowest moment of intoxicated degradation. I tugged at Rhonda's sequined pencil skirt and she tumbled towards me. I could feel consoling warmth, generated from the aroma of Harry, Rhonda's mink.

"This is certainly what you don't want to hear, honey. But the rat bastard ninny is not worth your tears. You can do better. Perhaps you can start hanging out at more places of satanic worship? I heard they like Cubans."

"I love you mother, but this is one of those

last straws where you just give up and decide your typical way of undoing a broken heart is outdated."

I felt an uncontrollable loneliness, ignoring the bobbing heads of consoling rhetoric that encircled me on the steps of Dick's. I felt the loneliness alongside the sensation of a drill having its way with my lower intestines. I sunk in a sudden heartbreak, feeling weak and bereft of autonomy.

"Be glad it may be over because it never would have lasted. Peck at the saving graces that you can gather from this romance you're so unfortunately good at ignoring. If something works only when you're blown out, it's just not worth it dear," Spike recited, as we sat on the ground, facing a twinkling Empire State Building.

Hints of trash ran alongside Avenue A, and Spike exhaled cigarette smoke into the light fixture outside of Dick's. I leaned my forehead against the pavement and heard my heart become louder as the drugs festered and I cowered inward, in a fetal position.

"It's just hard to accept that I can only connect with a sex partner when we're blown out."

"Human interaction under blow is such a mind fuck. And when the love is all over, you either keep doing it, or you stop and eventually make it out alive. Time heals the fucking wounds, you know?"

"Or you die."

"True."

"Unfortunately, my arteries were being stabbed by all the sweet nothings whispered by the sober lips of Broc Smith into some girl's ear who wasn't me. I feel used, like a cheap escapade fueled by drugs and sex, rather than a legitimate romance. Even though I know this relationship was, after all, my terrible idea. I didn't have to make out with him that one time."

"Reel it in girl. Living your life isn't a crime."

* * *

I drank consecutive martinis in a stewing rage. I walked into the bathroom stall and did enough cocaine to kill the misleading sense of love that's assisted by moderate snorting. I did enough to become a terrible human being, forgetting the potency of future loves, forgetting the worth of vulnerability and tenderness. Compromising every sincere connection to myself, blood from my nostrils settled on my top lip. I was no longer defenseless and no longer earnest, but a little squirmy mass of antagonism that cultivated anger enough for the entire universe.

"Fuck you for using me; for taking years of healing and placing me back in square one of self-hate. I hate you. Go love some other girl, see if I fucking care," I yelled into Smith's voicemail, unashamed of potential consequences, and well aware that we were never monogamous in the first place. Well aware I never even told him about Randall, about my libido, and about my heart's past. I was a liar, fabricating stories, scavenging for little tokens of justification.

For days I was a living corpse, starving for a bump, a hit, or a fix of anesthetized comfort. Eventually, I opened my safe of bullshit lists, dead ends and pulled out a photo of Enrique, a photo of my family, and the last photo of Randall I owned, after burning the rest. Cross-legged on the bathroom floor, I cried for hours, in the hollow depths beneath the Brooklyn–Queens Expressway. I pulled out the last bit of coke I had inside my back pocket, drew a line on my bathroom counter, sulked in discontent, and, for a minute, forgot what the point to all this was anyway.

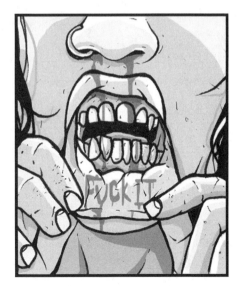

"We need to talk." Smith sounded more concerned than angry in the voicemail he left me in return.

I studied his voice, preparing myself for the confrontation. I was good at confrontation, until hormones enveloped the difficult exposure, and I started crying. That week, I got on a 6 train to Harlem. Smith lived on the seventh floor of an apartment building that smelled like fresh latex paint and black bean porridge smeared on the spoons of a Dominican kitchen. The smell of Spanish food diverted me and I felt an inner safety. However, walking up these same steps a week ago meant a subtle burning between my legs and up my nostrils, while tonight it meant a burning in my heart. I knew

I was lying when I claimed I was emotionally capable of being in this frivolous, endowed-by-drugs relationship.

Up the stairwell, to the seventh floor, I convinced myself that this wasn't going to be painful. Smith opened the door with a piercing smile and a cigarette dangling off the side of his lips. I offered him expensive shrink-wrapped snacks I shoplifted from a bodega en route to his apartment. He obliged with a mystical sincerity that almost fooled me into thinking make-up sex would ensue. We sat on opposite ends of his bedroom facing one another as excuses and explanations exited his lips. I told him nearly everything. Love that wasn't mutual had to reach its termination.

"You look different," Smith commented.

"I don't want to talk about it."

Four or five days ago, on the last morning I awoke beside Smith, the sun cracked our skulls as a brush of light killed our unconsciousness. We kissed each other's mouths and each other's organs. Blow-job after hand-job, we licked one another's unmentionable fluids that tasted like morning. Sweaty and unashamed, Smith commented on how delicious my insides were. Unaware of harm's tender hands reaching out to us from the distance, we tried to fuck for the first time, but I was unbearably tired. With a quiet determination to fuck him later in life, I exited his apartment, sucked dry and jittering with glee.

But on this night of conviction, an hour had passed and Smith walked me down to the stoop, away from the seventh floor, down into a paradox that would either set me free or add more bullshit to the list.

I had lied when I said I was incapable of developing feelings for someone I didn't even know that well, let alone under sober terms. I wanted Smith more than he wanted me, more than just a practical sex partner with the dialect of a sex therapist. *False hope burned us the hardest*, I thought, as I reached out my hand hoping a high-five would hurt less than an embrace. It could have been the last day of winter, or the first day of spring—I forget—but dirty mounds of snow and ice melted steadily on the cement while Smith held me, and I drew lines on the concrete with winter's unfortunate debris. It wasn't so bad, except when I realized yet another effort at connection had gone whistling past me.

CHAPTER TWELVE

As nudity raged on South Beach,
I foraged in a public school system
with an abstinence-only sex curriculum.

"Girl, you would have found him boring anyway, don't sweat it. And get home already," Luis consoled me on the telephone, after an offhand comment about Smith slipped from my mouth as I took the bus home the day after we severed ties.

"Damn, what a drama queen," the man sitting behind me whispered to another man next to him. I rolled my eyes and ignored him.

"I just miss getting to bang all the time."

"Oh, girl. You'll get over it. I'll see you later," Luis said with mild laughter and I hung up the phone.

"Damn. Now she's a ho," the same man remarked to the other man, according to the rules of turn-of-the-century etiquette, and I exited the bus.

I always tried to convince myself that the double standard between men and women as regards expressing one's loins' desire could not have survived in Brooklyn in the twenty-first century. But in fact, I always felt someone watching me from a hidden scaffolding, laughing, as "slut" and "whore" crept out from mouths of pedestrians. I gazed upon street lamps and vinyl signs, taxi rims and dreary-eyed vendors, and hoped for something in my city to say, "Yes, Virginia, fuck." As I walked to my front door, cozy smells of grilled beef empanadas danced like lines up my nostrils.

I never really knew Cuban sexuality, I thought, associating food and sex—my two most common bodily desires. Within my culture, sex was uncomfortably taboo. And for most of my life, all I could see were tumbleweeds on the road to sexual self-discovery. Damn, I'm glad I bailed from Miami.

Picking my nose as if gold sat in my temples, I thought of the parts of

my blood that were constructed of a gorgeous revolution. Made of tropical plants and percussion instruments, my blood made me proud, almost arrogant. Family reunions were moments to digress from my atypical life and reinvest, plentifully, in my culture, without political drama and irresponsible men. In my family, authority was possessed by women. In Miami, Cubans were both proud Latin immigrants (or the children thereof), and obnoxious right-wing conservatives, assimilated to a tee. Whether liberal or fundamentalist, rich or poor, the norm was to choose abstinence over condoms, so I was stuck. Whether it was Catholicism or bad taste that developed the sexual psyche Cuban-Americans coddled, I felt everyone should just get the fucking hell over it. Because I knew my people, in our precious island a few miles south, were happily raging at public parks.

There's no such thing as a flawless civilization, but nonetheless, I thought the entire Caribbean had been spoon-fed genetic glory by the tree gods of Mesopotamia, before the plates beneath each island shifted into individual territories. *I just adore those damn roots so fucking much*, I thought to myself. The more distant I felt from Miami, the less of a person I felt, no matter how accepted I was by another American city. One thing that all Cuban-Americans still have in common is the fact that going to visit our distant relatives isn't always financially possible, can't be a lighthearted holiday vacation. I don't like the embargo, I don't like Fidel, I don't like any government that at any point has criminalized human nature or repressed its people sexually or ethnically. But governments change. I try to remain hopeful. I guess for now, I'm stuck here in America, with an empty wallet, and no easy way of contacting the people from my motherland, because in the '60s, two assholes couldn't shut up, suck each other off, and prioritize human rights over their lofty dreams of world domination.

In Miami, we had our Christmas lights on all year. We ate dinner at 9 PM. We mopped the floor with a *palo de trapear* instead of a mop. Men didn't really wear shirts. People played dominoes at 2 AM, and despite the constant outrage exiting our mouths, we just wanted to survive. Piss broke, alright, well-off, or whatever. It was lovely. Humble. Special. But for some reason, I still felt like the only female in my family who was as in love with getting off as I was with my culture.

Instead of investigating healthy approaches to express my overactive libido as a teenager, I inherited the tact you'd expect from a society in which giving away condoms was frowned upon. I developed the nerve to combat my desires by joking senselessly of sluts. I paraded my distaste for sluts, and felt remorse for such hatred internally. Self-pity developed when my ethnic group affirmed my grotesqueness based on how many dicks I'd sucked and the fact that all genders aroused me. Self-pity inhabited my skull when even members of my supposed progressive and alternative scene assumed the same. Eventually I realized a functioning libido was a sign of good health;

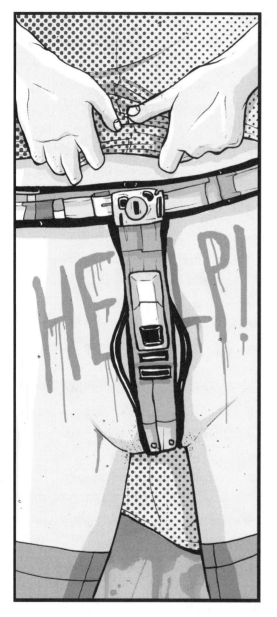

embracing safe sex, with or without a ball and chain, was *healthy*. And most people want to fuck.

Self-deprecation waned as I turned the key to enter my house. I'd forever be a tumbling byproduct of the aforementioned refutation, though, at the time, I would have liked for my soul to approve of my hormones a bit more generously.

The assimilation I'd undergone, to assist my otherworldly desires, burned a little hole the size of a cranberry in whatever Cuban matter was left in my soul. Remembering the present tense and easing up into my bedroom, I thanked the unmentionable heavens for basing my American assimilation on perversion and promiscuity, as opposed to prudish conservatism. And while the Cuban Right was ruling South Florida, I stayed in Brooklyn, where I had Christmas lights on all year, and where I hardly wore a shirt, despite my gender.

CHAPTER THIRTEEN

Revelation in a battery-operated phallus
and a pretty girl's handshake.

APRIL

My fantasy of revitalizing vaginal orgasms had finally come to pass but that afternoon in March, it sat there, defeated, in shambles on the floor of my bedroom. The fabricated ambition of love burned me beneath the wings of the cocaine angels; yet my bad habits burned too. And while the sex ended, the exploration of biology and vulnerability never could. It was almost spring. A month-long cocaine low had passed. I had finally begun saving money after consecutive splurges, and I felt detached from the battered little journey with my burning little peach, a journey I was so set on concluding.

Sex wasn't going to be a vision quest, but an activity to get lost in. I wanted to tend to that G-spot more than ever and for once, in adulthood, my reproductive insides felt sixteen. The season of rebirth was tumbling over, and I could hear the pussy cats in heat, pacing frantically up and down Humboldt Avenue. Birds, roommates, neighbors, rats, and pigeons found harbor in walls, as did circus freaks, criminals, and the elderly who were all, in unison, rejoicing for the season of sexual revival, where everyone's survival was defined by the caliber of an orgasm. Tiny hints of foliage peeked through the stems of the trees blossoming from out of the concrete dugout behind the door in my bedroom. Drafts of cold still entered through the cracks around the door, so

I lay on my bed and hid my wilted body beneath a couple of black wool sheets.

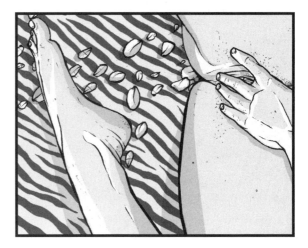

Lying on my bed, ruminating over that tantalizing discovery I had made—that good sex can exist—I decided to re-discover, alone, an organ that catered perfectly to such desires. I swerved up and down a pair of labia that seemed to have more patience than I could ever dream of. My right hand diverted itself to my left tit; the supple mound of nerves jiggled delicately, as my hips thrust from the mattress to mid-air. Side A of the record I was listening to was almost done, as I created a great body of water between my legs; a hot spring the likes of which no lover had ever seen. As the backyard embers smelled more and more like the ever-complex weather patterns of the North, I panicked for a minute, because I hated getting up to flip the record

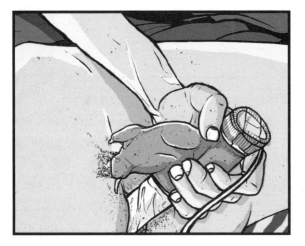

when I masturbated. The last track began and my thoughts were reinvested in my groin. My hands brushed themselves against the sheets and pillows, wiping an excess of holy water. Groping at the stash beneath my one velvet pillow with the pretty golden tassels, I took a dildo and I fucked myself hard. Moaning at the volume of the last song on the record that played, I reached a pinnacle so biologically pure and self-ruling, the spoiled debris of hard love and hard drugs dissipated at a manic pace. The tunnel between my ovaries and the prosperity of the outside world shone with a dazzling new light, as I found my vagina again.

Throughout the smoothest rotation a battery-operated dildo/clit-tickler combo could offer, sounds shifted from the end of my record, to my lips in an untamed rapture, to the noise upstairs; Spike was spinning Iron Maiden. It blasted through my ceiling as an epic praise to my new love, self-exploration.

I had an orgasm, Bruce Dickinson wailed my organ's new accidental anthem, and spring had finally begun.

With time, Smith became less of a potential love who didn't want me, and more like just another friend who bruised my vulnerabilities while rewarding my libido. The result was a nudge to stop using drugged lovers for the sake of my own self-learning; it was enough to dissolve most regrets entangled with a saga about love and cocaine. Smith became less like a rigid crown molding and more like a crane, attacking my baggage and refurbishing my insides.

I walked into the living room to find Luis, RJ, and Spike all sitting around Marilyn, Consuela's replacement. They looked up and smiled.

"You know I heard that performance, girl, and I must say, you would make a great Broadway star," Luis commended.

"Oh thank you darling, I thought I might have sounded a bit rusty. I was, after all, a bit clogged around the pipes."

"Maybe you can fall in love one day," RJ interjected.

"Yeah. I just have to learn how to get broken up with."

*   *   *

I received a postcard from Tatiana soon after. She would be in New York City the weekend after the date on the postcard. I awaited her arrival with the sense of a looming rebound from Smith, and of course the possibility of falling in love with her.

*   *   *

I awoke the morning of her arrival, daydreaming of our marriage: *Tatiana's pinstripe slacks, jet-black fedora, and red and black striped tie looked darling beside my leopard print pencil skirt. All of our friends mingled with our proud mothers and fathers, exuding such warmth we were wondering why we ever thought coming out would be so difficult. Mashed potatoes, fried sweet potatoes, chimichurri, mofongo, and a six-foot paella adorned the wooden planks of the*

138

reception hall, and gave off the most perfect smell of Latin and southern cuisine. Tatiana grabbed my waist as we kissed. Bruce Dickinson announced us bride and bride, and hand in hand we ran toward the street where the leather seats of Tatiana's Triumph Bonneville awaited our plump, newlywed asses.

In mid-thought, Tatiana knocked on my door. Her eyes lit up beneath a knitted hat that exposed several loose strands of black hair. Her nose was red and weathered, and her lips, soft and well taken care of. Tatiana was a lovely firecracker with little shuffling feet that lifted her as she walked. She was the only member of her family with green eyes. She entered my living room, took a hit off Marilyn, and told me stories until four o'clock in the morning.

"You only wear one shirt," I told her, with a smile paralyzing my face. Tatiana had on a Spitfire Skateboards t-shirt, the only one I ever remember her wearing.

"I miss skateboarding. The accident killed me."

"At least you have that shirt."

"Yeah."

*   *   *

That night, Tatiana lay next to me and we looked at one another, suspecting the unreciprocated nature of our whirlwind feelings teetering between lust and companionship.

"I care about you a lot," she said to me.

"I care about you too."

"I know how you feel, but I want to stay friends."

"I do too. I can. Don't worry about me."

"So tell me if I'm ever crossing any emotional boundaries. I don't know. Punch me in the face or something," Tatiana said to me before kissing my cheek and shutting off the lights. We nearly passed out, and slept an arm's

length away from each other. I woke up alone. I looked over to the other end of the room, and Tatiana was slurping on a cup of coffee while packing her belongings.

"Yo girl, what's up with the guy next door?" Tatiana asked laughing.

"What guy?"

"The dude at the bodega. He keeps asking me if I'm staying with the gay people. I told him I was staying with the clowns. Isn't that funny?"

"He probably just wants to know if you're gay too 'cause he wants ass. He's alright once you see him every day of your life."

"Oh damn."

"You should talk to him in Spanish, he'll tell you secrets. He only *thinks* he's a homophobe."

"Well. At least he's obviously in love with me."

"I don't blame him." Tatiana threw a bag of dinner rolls at my face. I rolled over towards the wall and she went upstairs for an hour of hygiene.

*   *   *

Tatiana was going home so I walked her to the door and embraced her. We stood there as the sounds of trucks drowned our small voices, as RJ walked beside us complaining about the smell of piss entering the living room, and as Spike arrived home, asking me to pack Marylin's bowl as soon as possible because he thought he might have crabs. It was all so unfortunately tragicomical. Luis cooked a steak as Tatiana's little vegetarian nostrils sought purer oxygen. A pigeon shat beside Tatiana's little boots. On my front step that morning, everything that could kill a moment was welcome.

But in a brush of sincerity, the moment entailed every truth I wanted to believe. Tatiana wasn't a manifestation of Randall, my father, or any asshole who ever broke up with me by ignoring my existence. History doesn't really repeat itself that often, the way karmic revelations have made me believe. Tatiana was not coming back as the manifestation of new love, but in whatever way she could. Because she said she cared, and I believed her.

CHAPTER FOURTEEN

The promised land.

APRIL

"**S**hoot the Freak," said the sign at Coney Island, on a strip of land that faced the boardwalk and the Atlantic Ocean. The slogan gave me terrible thoughts, even though the sign itself was festive, antique, and made me smile. In these thoughts, all self-proclaimed freaks ran for their lives while leaders of chic development shot at them with 1000-mile-per-hour bullets. The corpses of visionaries were then spread in the playing field, piled lifeless, in the name of tourism. Our angels' wings were a strategic collage of debris upon debris—art made out of tin cans, cigarette butts, pamphlets, receipts, ride tickets, and other odd paper goods. Encrusted with

a paint job of the blackest blood known to human flesh, the angels danced. *What else is there to do when your home is destroyed?* they asked one another. The wings sparkled, but nobody who possessed the power to destroy Coney Island seemed to care for their gold detailing and handsome construction. Soon, the thought would end and I would take a look, as if it were my last, at Coney Island.

I wasn't even from New York or any of its neighboring regions. But I couldn't help it when I fell in love with Coney Island, a financially fragile and socially heated strip of sand, cement, and magical assemblies. I experienced a foolish and unsuspecting love at first sight. Once I'd discovered it, I tried to remodel every room in my house as a replica of Coney Island's structural inhabitants. Perhaps I was just tapping into my inner tortured idiot, because I studied her, and was enamored of her without even knowing her, let alone having been a part of her life during her most severe changes.

I didn't know what the residents of Coney Island wanted out of their homes. But I also didn't believe in our nation's model of rehabilitation—smash the past, polish class, exterminate ethnic and economic diversity, and rebuild. My desires weren't selfish, I hoped. I wasn't against a transformation, if such a thing were to reward the region and its people. Change sounded delightful, if it would negate the possibility of Coney Island tumbling into a hapless Armageddon where no one would mind the ruins—they'd just rot, and be used for free summer concerts no one attends.

Development and progress are alright, when they assist what exists, not destroy it. The painted signs and the nice vendors preserved the grit and splendor of New York City twenty years in retrospect. I didn't want to romantically recreate the past; it was just difficult to watch the most beautiful eras die, slowly and surely.

On the first day of Coney Island season, I watched from the Wonder Wheel two times in a row, dreading that blow where Astroland would surrender to purity and allow its crumbling statues to be defiled. The blow lay in

the distance though, so I sat cross-legged in a little white cage hovering above the Atlantic coast with a half-smile. *Fragility begets beauty*, I thought. It's why ruins become art and love only begins to make sense when in peril.

From my Wonder Wheel cage I hoped for just a little more change and a less tragic blow. Of course, every now and then, I sobbed over the dead end of my hopes for Tatiana. But I was willing and enthused to embrace any kind of climactic change, despite how unskilled I was at neglecting my emotions. Change was constant, in the brain and the reconstructing of self-esteem, in the rehabilitation of vices, and in the urge to salvage the paint chips slowly falling off the shafts of the Wonder Wheel. The sun will continue setting in the west and rising in the east. We'll watch it from a derailed boardwalk and forget how construction scarred the tissue of a town's character, because at that moment, the sun looks beautiful.

I stared from my little white cage, regarding a brittle strip of land that propped itself on poles made of eggshells. New Yorkers, like antique structures, were eternally in line for an internal cleansing. For the time being, I accepted my recent misfortunes in order to set off for the bullets of the future. I was protective of my experiences and how I chose to let them touch me. I was protective of my home, my routine, my local dives and humble watering holes, and how the United States of America touched us. Misfortune will laugh at me in retrospect through a pack of bloodthirsty canines, which appear and reappear as the most random manifestations of varying types of pain.

How do I accept such an inescapable facet of life? Misfortune. I analyzed misfortune itself, as the Wonder Wheel rotated towards the clouds and an early moon. Misfortune seemed like something you can only make the best of once the rest of your wounds are scabbing and something reminds you that you are worth the rehabilitation.

CHAPTER FIFTEEN

The dawning of the age of 'shroom season.

MAY

O n an overcast afternoon, the doorbell rang, and I opened it.
"Hey, are you here to fix my computer?" I asked the guy standing on the other side of the door.

"Yeah. I'm Ashby. Calvino Ashby. Hammertoe's friend. Do you have coffee?"

"No, but I have beer."

A mutual friend told Ashby that my computer was in peril. His enthusiastic interest in fixing my machine free of charge, perhaps for peculiar shits and giggles, baffled me. Humans aren't inherently nice, I believed, in this city where impersonal energy is rampant in tight spaces. But I acted as if such kindness was completely normal. Ashby's nose sloped in the way I liked. He looked ten years younger than his actual age and always seemed as if he had somewhere else to be—not because he looked bored, but because he always looked lost, and I found that endearing. Showing scant interest in leaving my apartment, we talked in circles, and I sought answers. *Who the fuck is Calvino Ashby and why is he in my house, giving off a boisterous aroma of roasted garlic and a long jog? Why doesn't Calvino Ashby ever walk in a straight line?* I asked myself and stared with deeper intent.

"So . . . do you like musicals?" I asked him, expecting a miracle.

"No."

"Oh."

"I mean yeah, I love them."

"Really?"

"Yeah. I'm serious though, I really like *South Pacific* in a way that doesn't make sense to that many people."

"Me too." Ashby sat beside me as I doodled mindlessly on a piece of paper. His fingers were nimble, and robust in the parts where strength was desirable. Ashby fidgeted with the electronics sitting on a neon pink wooden desk and I watched periodically, taking note of the shape of his mouth.

"So how can I pay you?" I asked him, after the computer was repaired.

"Do you know where I can find hallucinogenic mushrooms?"

"Ha." I was enthralled. "I can buy you some. The only problem with that, however, is that you would have to enter, you know, the third realm with me. On my roof. Tomorrow."

"Sounds good."

"I can't tonight. I have a date with someone I don't really like."

"Me too." We stared blankly at one another.

"So, have you heard *Judy Speaks*? It's Judy Garland's spoken word confessional," I asked.

"God, are you trying to get me to like you or something?"

"And who the fuck are you?"

*

ONE WEEK LATER

I always crushed on Howard Hughes. A handsome, tortured genius with a shameless adoration for speed and tits. I could mentally probe him, and sink, vicariously, into the moments when one can hardly fret over the loss of emotional capacity and thousands of dollars, because you're finally seeing your dreams come to fruition. But as capable and perfect as that speed feels—as that love feels—your insanity silences you, your utter brilliance a stigma. But apparently sick people are good at something. Speed? Passion? Who the fuck needs cocaine when the spark is so biologically fateful?

* * *

I arrived in Brooklyn from running errands in Manhattan in a childish rage one Sunday afternoon. Shaking in my shoes at the front door, I asked myself, *Will this be another droll, dead-end, manic June ending in fierce self-loathing? Or a new kind of love fabricated with warm interactions and an ever-flowing relationship with my organs?* Like Isabelle said, too long ago to even remember exactly what she predicted.

Spike waltzed into my room at midnight, hands cupped above his mouth and pouncing lightly on his feet.

"Do you want to trip on mushrooms with me? There is an ounce in my bag and for some reason it's not in my mouth."

"I guess I got enough work done in the last four hours." I was freelance writing at the time. "And I guess I'm tired of the color scheme of this whole motherfucking neighborhood." I took a drag off a cigarette and considered my options. "And I guess I can say I'm happily devoted to fitting bigger objects in my tang." I stared deeply into Spike's eyes. "But it has been a long time coming. And that may throw me to the dark side." I look down at the doughnut. "But it is a new season. And I guess I need to initiate that somehow."

"And face the dark side," Spike recited.

"To us!" I bellowed as Spike held a donut filled with strawberry jelly and psilocybin mushrooms in the air. After several minutes, the colors began coagulating into a collaged mess, and the objects began morphing into sculptures from either fifty years ago or outer space. My visual perception had changed a little ever since that acid we did in Miami—not necessarily

in the most comfortable way, but I knew it was temporary. In moments such as this, I felt like a pubescent rebel, a fiend for new discovery. Were chemical trips channeling new beginnings, or was I fabricating turning points with chosen hallucinogenic trips in order to assemble my life with over-stimulating chapter openers? I didn't care, I thought. I was ecstatic for the moment. I was hardly manic, but dying for reinvention.

"Did you know I gave Ashby a blow job?" I told Spike.

"Oh yeah? That is really nice. It's nice to answer to your genitals every now and then."

"Sometimes they just need to stop asking for so much, though."

"Oh honey that is *your* problem that you want dick *and* vagina."

"Yeah, I'm an asshole I guess."

*   *   *

Hours of frolicking resumed, until we entered the final portal of our alternate universe and began an unfortunate comedown. There exists a moment in every hallucinogenic trip when I decide to want everything I can't have. At around midnight that Sunday, salt was too bitter and sugar burned my tongue with an acidic tinge that killed the roof of my mouth. My teeth slowly detached themselves from my nerves' endings and I could unfortunately feel my arms again. Everything resembled filth and the pulsing of sheets and furniture was no longer a theatrical display, but an annoying inconvenience, which in my mind somehow paralleled the destruction of the universe. I peeled layer after layer of dirt and sweat off my skin. I tried to paint solace with it but instead I made streak after streak of garbage and despair until I felt an inner romance with anger. The same anger that I was taught to ignore because I had tits and a pussy. The anger felt appropriate, and I basked in its honesty with a loving sense of malice.

"I WANT TO FALL IN LOVE AGAIN AHHHHH AHHHHH," I yelled to Spike in an intoxicated rage.

Then I had a realization—that a good lover, a destructive bender, or a bottle of pills may pick up some loose ends, but wars still run rampant whether or not we take note of them. Our only choice is to trudge valiantly and figure shit out in the least destructive way possible. We fumble night and day for that serenity that only exists in short spurts of sanity and beauty; those biological spurts of love, unassisted by drugs, that happen imperfectly, but often.

Love couldn't possibly be pure in a story with one lover, I thought, as visions of Isabelle danced in my head. I began preaching aloud, standing on a coffee table, in another fake accent.

"Because nothing can be pure. Everything ends, and sometimes, it's supposed to. Nothing can be flawless, unless you choose to be blind to disaster." Spike nodded in agreement. "Like people who pretend everything's actually okay 'cause they have a nice house, two-point-five children, and an SUV. In their brains, blindness wraps itself; they deny their true desires, and for some reason, they're never fucking happy. 'Cause they never took a motherfucking risk."

"Safety only works when you don't mind dying alone," Spike said as he lay on the ground.

"Come sit with me on this pile of clear sludge." We sat on a white comforter and stopped talking for a second. I rethought desire, and dreamed of the risks I took in order to dabble in love, lust, and all the harmful toxins in between.

I began to calculate the math of death: you live for a while, then you die forever. I wanted to make something of this life—this microscopic splurge with destruction, which only lasts about twenty-seven or eighty-seven years, and looks pathetic in the grand scheme of infinity. Christianity says everything

may just as well be shit until it dies, if our purpose is to die without sin and end up in heaven for infinity—the epoch we're *supposed* to be living for. I, however, begged to differ regularly, and frolicked alongside sin recklessly.

On that night, I was proud and I felt accomplished. I stopped caring so much about "the answers." I was just fine with the pint of Guinness Spike poured into a glass for me. I was fine with Aerosmith's greatest hits spinning, and the eager soul I had somehow brought to life.

Spike flipped on the fog machine. We danced between its hollow clouds of smoke and a green light bulb, in order to create the trippiest effect possible, when all you have are rotting party bulbs, left over from parties, and two pounds of dry ice.

"Maybe you can make a love story after all?" Spike concluded.

"No, I think love will just be a hallucination." I was a jaded old maid.

"At least we didn't get chased into the ocean by freaks this time."

"Nope. Just flying through space."

"We're doin' better than Howard Hughes ever did."

"Totally."

CHAPTER SIXTEEN

Might as well.
We're all fucked up already anyway.

JUNE

Every flow of electricity existing in the form of clocks and watches said to me: *fast-forward emotion and neglect the past*. Mistakes had become fractures, and lost love was a mere wrinkle in the salty drape of life. Looking back, my heart in a shambles looked good on every night of catastrophe. Crying over Sally, Smith, and whoever-the-fuck over on 6TH and Avenue B or A or 3RD or whatever. It actually felt good to feel something every now and then, I learned through the hypersensitivity between tragedy and dullness. Feelings awoke my hidden vulnerabilities and with every unfortunate tear running down my cheek, I learned something new. It's good to feel *something*, I thought. Even if it was a peculiar, yet good feeling, generated by another human being.

* * *

"What's behind that wall?" Ashby and I were lying on my bed, in the basement. We had just argued, for the first time. I was on the twenty-eighth day of my cycle.

"The boiler room. I like it. You know, it makes comforting noises. All our shit is in there."

"Does your landlord know?"

"Yeah. And if because of our shit, one day, something explodes—we'll be the first to die." Ashby looked at me and I'm not sure if he thought I was breathtaking or insane, but fighting felt easy with him. We could divert the conversation into a pile of jargon that, for some reason, intrigued us both. He was from the Bronx and he was pretty crazy, like me.

On a morning after my graveyard shift at the bar on 2ND Avenue, we had been bickering together on the train and my bed. I hated him for a few hours and couldn't understand how a date on a mushroom trip could even become this, this consistency of good and bad, but mostly good. I didn't believe in prosperity and questioned myself continually. *Can I even trust you? You're a man.* All lovers quarrel, and then they burn. But when a conflict existed over inescapable feelings, we couldn't hate each other, only acknowledge and understand the wars that brought us to the battleground where we confronted one another naked, crying on my bed. Human conflict undressed our vulnerabilities and everyday we undressed. Concealing my bare emotions from someone who's woken up next to me for days in a row was surprisingly difficult. Ashby turned to me and regurgitated all inner portals of his brain; dissecting all woes, dirty thoughts, past loves, and concealed obsessions. The fire lessened and we thumbed through photographs.

"Isn't she fucking hot?" Ashby pointed to a picture.

"Yeah I would fuck her."

"Yeah you would totally fall in love with her if you met her."

"I don't know about that, I might just fuck her."

"I'm a skeptic too." Ashby stared at the photos in my hands.

"Here is a picture of Randall. What a fucking waste. All I can remember of him was his terrible gigantic cock. If only he would have known how to use it. If only he would have been older."

"You can handle a dirty old man, can you?"

"The older they are, the more times they've fucked up enough to know a little more about themselves . . . how to use their large penises."

Ashby and I drained the blood out of things I had questioned for ages; about people I thought I might be able to love. He lay next to me and put his hand on my stomach, pricking the ends of my worst nerves. We drank a forty, fell asleep, woke up, cleaned my period off our woes, and drank something fluorescent and caffeinated for determination. We walked down to the

train and took it to the coast. As it exited our neighborhood and ran above ground, cemeteries sprawled, and whatever we could see of the sun started going down.

"I'm not really that scared to die I guess," I told him, leaning against the doors.

"You just want it to happen the right way."

"A hot air balloon."

"I'll probably poison myself by mistake."

"You won't die of that. Am I dying right now? By hanging out with you?"

"I know, right?"

"Hopefully this doesn't kill us before the boiler room does." Ashby smiled and stood behind me, palms pressed against the window. We watched the cemeteries, factories, and ruins pass by as I laid my head on his chest.

*   *   *

Alone at dusk, we went to a beach hardly anybody visited, at least on wet, overcast weekdays at happy hour. Surrounded by aluminum cans, and with well-pressed spliffs between our lips, we sat on rocks facing the horizon. Only fog, riptides, and dusty particles from our hazy visions resided in the distance. He got up, cracked his knuckles and breathed deeply, pacing frantically, but succumbed to a warm zeal for life. He walked towards me, where the sand was damp enough to feel like concrete. Patting his chest and exhal-

ing, he touched me on the shoulders.

"I fucking love life right now," he crooned, and I was close to agreeing.

Cranially dissecting how it feels to love without any chemical push, I felt it begin to rain. We walked towards civilization and the sultry sounds of damp socks exited my feet, reeking of recklessness and sex. The hairs on my arms stood in pleasant disarray and I felt prickly and diseased; it was the good kind of dirty. Swaying with wide steps, like lost beasts in the wilderness, we walked around, fucked up on life, with a different energy than the kind you got from acid, coke, or New York City.

* * *

JULY

I always just kind of thought sex would be okay if everyone's intentions were out in the open—if everyone involved had a boner. If everyone was awake, in love, almost in love, or at least enamored with one another. This way, sex hardly hurt. And for the sake of my uncontrollable breath palpitating with the act of romantically sucking this dick, I shouldn't really have imagined why *sex could be wrong*.

*   *   *

It almost felt like I had salvaged my well-being. It had been a while since I felt fragility when I kissed someone. Sexuality was no longer destructive, desperate, coked, and unwise. Not an aimless trek intended to erase memories that impeded my human progress so much that it was hard to give a fuck about any of this. I had just been blindly foraging through a lovely moment in time, in which all that mattered was how good something in me felt. Something I saw almost every day. And it hadn't been a spark of determination that existed as air in me, but an actual body part. A body part not my own, but someone else's; someone whose dick was nestled at ease inside my mouth, while we lay on my sheets that were stained with wax from melting candles, and beer from toppled cans.

*   *   *

There was this dull, raggedy man named Bruce I knew in South Florida whom I used to get into fights with every day. He once said that it was more radical to forget what falling in love felt like. To live your life free of any emotional ball and chain. To subdue weakness when you begin to feel love for another human being. I thought, *in that case, would it be revolutionary to recall only pain?*

Discarding a potentially weakening pleasure like love, dancing, or smoking marijuana, before it ever destroyed me, was useless. I thought of myself when I was unhappy, drowning in a wealth of consecutive dead ends, with bottled emotions so large the glass made dents on my skin. I thought of how incapable I was of doing anything I believed in then—*how can that be radical? Constantly taking note of the deadly triggers of our humble world may swell defenses indefinitely, but a fair acceptance of happiness is crucial to anyone's ability to function, especially anyone who's seen writing on their forehead that says, PLEASE KILL ME,* I thought to myself on that day with Bruce, looking at several little green parrots that gathered on the pick-up truck facing us.

I didn't fight with Bruce that time, though. He really wanted to be in love. He missed the girl who cheated on him when she fucked his friend. He forgave her and everything. She didn't fuck his friend because she was a terrible person, but she was just heading in a slightly different direction than when Bruce had first met her. Bruce and I fought about men and women and society and gay people. That conservative Neanderthal motherfucker—I could tell he was a frail guy anyway. I was frail too, I realized. With all this new commotion and possibility for love. But for fragility, it was pretty fucking beautiful that time.

CHAPTER SEVENTEEN

Content and disorderly.

AUGUST

Without taking note of time, wasting days in Spike's rusty Jeep listening to reggae and complaining about money, one thing led to another and Dust was shutting down on a Tuesday night in August. Drunkards swayed and blown-out motherfuckers wrestled with reality through the kindest, friendliest handshakes I had felt in years. Rhonda seemed to be on stilts, but it was only radiance, towering above the wig that had often carried on much later than the people at Dust. But we danced as if it were any other night. We got drunk, as if it were any other night. No one spoke a word of remorse, and I hid behind the pleasant goggles of companionship. I was sad this little moment of thrill that my friends were paid to do was done. It wasn't about paying the bills by playing records or about getting free liquor, but about the several hours each week when the world was devoid of rampant loathing. It was about mental and physical rehabilitation. In the end, everyone was a bit of a mess, but nobody cried or anything. We just, well, carried on, like good wigs.

While Dust was a sanctified temple in the civilization of New York City nightlife, I took pride in sticking till the end every night. But on the last night, Ashby and I took our worn-out delirium home earlier than everyone else. I felt like an asshole, but no one really minded, and I guess that's what friends are for. Sinking into the harmonic pulse from the subway tracks before a train arrived, Ashby embraced me and I hardly questioned the gesture.

To Ashby and me, it sometimes seemed as if everyone we knew was trying to recreate their youths in order to be happy. On our finer days, we sang songs, laughed, squinted at the city lights, and took pride in disassociating hope from youthfulness. Recreating our lighter years felt dull and useless, and

hope didn't need us. The utopian idea of love bored Ashby and me. Admittedly, it would have been easier if we were naïve, and love and marriage would suffice even if everything else was wrong, but we still lived under fire. Ashby still lived in my room, in the basement of the Palace beneath the expressway. I was still confused and irrational, and Ashby was still a mess—but for some reason, being together made us happy.

We arrived home as the sun peeked through an overcast mess hovering above Brooklyn. Scuffling under the sheets for Ashby's hands that night, I fell asleep while an inner victory made its way through my veins. My room had no windows—we worked temp jobs from home and bar jobs at twilight so the difference between day and night was hardly noticeable. I awoke in a cold sweat with my face nuzzled into Ashby's collarbone. I inhaled before consciousness struck me, and I smelled the splendor of a human body that lay on my sheets for the same reason I did. Our inland cave was home—our bodies were home. While we were awake, Ashby and I could tell each other anything. Hate and despair recklessly frolicked in the open and I lost the sense

of embarrassment that I too often tied to weakness. Vulnerabilities spread out naked, like our drunken bodies unconsciously tickling one another the morning after Dust's last fête.

One of Ashby's eyes slowly opened and caught me staring at the rise-and-fall of his chest as we both pretended to sleep. I peered at a clock and saw it was almost noon, the time most of us would insist on starting the day. Having no intention to push my life back into clockwork, I clenched the curve of his pelvic bone and slid my fingers up his side and above a subtle heartbeat. My leg slid upward, in unison with my hand, and I created a gentle sheath between his body and the suffocating air of the rest of the world. My heart paced frantically, and as my insides fully awoke, my sweaty limbs, in full consciousness, held the conscious body of Calvino Ashby. Our physical togetherness wasn't just a side effect of a binge up our nostrils. Ashby's hand rested on my head. Through my ceiling, we could hear the hustling bustle of Sinatra on vinyl, pacing leather boots, and hung-over voices. My hand diverted itself to Ashby's temples, and I kissed the opposite side of his jaw. Through the drywall papered in damask, the rats and pigeons gathered and comforted me.

*   *   *

When Ashby and I talked, he would correct my English grammar and I would correct his Spanish pronunciation. Ashby noticed the inventive shapes the sky made but when he walked on staircases, he only used every other step. And while I would be too busy feeling the breeze and the smog through my shirt collar to take notice of the sky, I noticed the accidental art made by cigarette butts and damp soil on every step of every staircase. One day the month before, we had sat and watched eighteen rides of the Cyclone at Coney Island. Eighteen thirty-second near-death experiences in a beautiful rickety mess of wood and iron where small people can rise to the occasion and die at the speed of light.

"I hate heights and drops without a nice seat-belt. I hate how my heart races while it flies above my face and my brain sinks to my feet if I'm not carefully tied up to something," I said.

"Another sip of this cocktail will kill your desire for safety."

"You know I would live on a roller coaster if it had a fat harness." I ignored him, while lying on a wooden picnic table accented with little fried trimmings that had fallen off the ends of chicken wings and knishes. "It's totally my favorite place to be." I took a drag off a spliff I had salvaged from RJ earlier that afternoon. "It's the only place where the scenery is moving as fast as my mind."

"Yeah. But then when it stops you're back to that monotony where settling down is the hardest shit in the world," Ashby said.

"Yeah. Settling down. How the fuck do people do that?"

"Do you ever just read a book, and not really pay attention to what's going on, but consciously read the words while you're thinking 'Alright now! I'm reading a book.'"

"Every fucking day."

*   *   *

I also hated feeling like I was going to die. I enjoyed some kinds of pain and gravitationally defiant movement only to the extent I considered it safe. I don't think many things will kill me, except perhaps a broken old roller coaster with no seat-belts and shitty lovers. Dying from what you love the most is the worst and best way to die. I hated the way my heart sank when I took chances with lovers and got nothing useful from the heartbreak beyond a few surly sentences on bitter love. But they hadn't killed me yet, I thought.

"Risks are worth taking in order to know if some fuck or some joyride is useless or not," Ashby said.

"Yeah, I'm just never that motivated to face things I might not enjoy" I took several sips from our drinks and we rode the Cyclone to watch my face sink into my neck. I dissected things in a way that I thought Ashby might hate, but for some reason, he put up with it. In other words, I talked a lot of shit. I sighed, smiled, and survived with a comforting sense of completion.

We sat on a couple of rocks, stared, kissed, and flirted with childish snarls. My hands clenched his ears, his hands clenched my hips, and we kissed for a while. There were some risks worth taking, and for the time being they had made us better. And if something, like a new love, provided us with anger or wisdom that fulfilled us in the long run, it was worth the chance of regret.

We got back on the train as onlookers sneered and I sighed. The beautiful mess that dragged us through, or pulled us out of, some of the hardest months of our lives survived for a while.

CHAPTER EIGHTEEN

Dabbling in sincerity—
another boring gamble.

W ith the end of summer came the time to crawl back into that cave of responsibility where there was too much to gather of ourselves before we began embracing any unkempt attempt at love.

"Let's ride bikes to Arizona," I told Ashby on my stairwell, as he was about to leave my house. He kissed me and ran his hand through the strands and curls performing in slippery disarray on my head. I looked up at his crystal green eyes and pulled him close. I didn't feel unconditional love, but I felt good about us. In a moment that, in my eyes, could catapult us into a future of possible love, or maybe even self-imposed monogamy, Ashby put me aside and we walked towards the front door. We walked through Brooklyn and ended up in an empty park.

"In order to ride out west we totally need fatter paychecks. And I need to get over my bullshit. While you get on with the end of yours. I guess it's time to find that stability and clarity that happens before and after fucking shit up," Ashby said.

"So you're gonna go, huh?"

"No, I mean, yeah. But I'm a fucking mess. Face it. I have to go, you know, get my shit together."

"Well that's overdue. But is it really that hard to find your life here? In Brooklyn?" I stopped smiling and looked at Ashby. Avoiding the truth that this discussion might be a hazardous precursor, I crossed my arms and sighed. "Will you be back? You know. When your dust settles in?"

"I want to have you in my life."

"How do you think it'll be?"

"Who the hell knows," Ashby said without self-righteousness. Feeling like failures at love, we faced one another and hashed out the truth that this utopian free-fall of romantic feelings wasn't going to save us from the rest of the world. In a moment when Ashby was determined to take care of himself, I needed to be selfish. At that minute, a packed and potent blunt was all I dreamed of having. But by 11 AM, on a patch of grass too far from my home, I remained herbally unaltered. Ashby and I popped two Adderalls to

calm us down. I was determined to say everything truth- fully, the way we did the day we met.

"I think I might fall in love with you," I said. The dialogue was read with calm- ness; but we nearly killed one another through a gripping, theatrical tug of war in which I pulled tears from his eye sockets and he made the color of my skin transcend into fury. I cried and yelled and tore grass from the ground. Ashby put his hands on his head and faced the ground without anger or retaliation. Without knowing what he might feel later or felt in the present, nothing exited his mouth.

"I'm not in love with you," Ashby relayed, after hours of outrageous sacrilege.

"I'm not in love with you either." Sometimes you don't know what comes out of your mouth when you want to say everything. "But I still want to touch you, every now and then, in a way I don't want to touch my other friends who I am not in love with either. And you say you don't want that, and I know and understand why. Because you have to get your shit together and a girlfriend doesn't technically fit into that process. But for some reason, my feelings persist, so it might get a little hard someday. I just need to be honest."

"I'm sorry. I really tried. But I can't invent love that I want so bad, yet don't feel, while the rest of my life wilts away without me. I think we both deserve to be in love and I don't understand what the fuck is wrong with me. Lacking any ability to feel passion like a motherfucking corpse."

I embraced him, he said goodbye, and I took a bus through Brooklyn and Queens for mental clarity. I felt an outrageous sense of isolation that I hadn't felt since my first love dumped me when I was eighteen—*being uncommitted for so many offbeat years was so much easier*, I thought. People break up, parents leave you without an explanation, and people fuck each other over in order to survive all the fucking time. Making sense of it through a method that gave us authority over our own bodies was the difficult part. Looking back, I appreciate the way my family didn't impose divorce details onto my typically baffled, developing brain. And my family's lack of interest in sexuality may have been some angel's gentle offering—which made it easier to ignore that they might, like their community, have had an intense distaste for unforgiving, sexually deviant, bisexuality. Hell, I don't even remember ever hating the first person who ever really broke my heart. Because in the end, monogamy at eighteen wasn't for me anyway.

For two hours of an aimless journey, it truly felt like the end of my life. I was immersed in pain that was almost comforting, in which a desperate longing for a lost love awoke my senses from neutrality. But I fucking hated it all. *When will I be manic and free again?* I prayed through the tainted windows of the bus, as it rode beneath the Brooklyn–Queens Expressway, alongside my street.

Ashby's current period of self-revelation echoed the year I had just overcome, but I, however, had to watch out for my health. I couldn't pretend knowing him wasn't sickly painful. I had to leave his side as the friend he adored, and I hated myself for it. But I was done probing my brain's malfunctioning parts. The idea of settling for what was left, without romance, killed me. I'm only human. I wasn't okay enough to have a friendship with someone I wanted to touch copiously, whether or not our bodies learned to need one another in other ways. In the end, we were all fuck-ups, hurting one another without wanting to. Feeling lost in the world we knew as home was, actually, enough to destroy any relationship.

The rest of autumn coddled us with good weather, but I could hardly see the good in anything. Ashby left on a temporary excursion. The situation left me with a choice: come off this splurge of unsuspected heartbreak during these months of depression with a new lightness, or prepare for a dreadful cycle of monotonous pain. Ashby, however, was hardly even gone. We were stuck in a sickening cul-de-sac, pulling one another closer while pushing one another away. Trying to retain the same outrageous level of connection with Ashby created false hope on my end, and death to unabashed sincerity on his. So I was annoying. I overanalyzed his letters. I wondered if there was something wrong with me, given that Ashby had several lengthy relationships before me, while I had just a couple of years of hitching across the country with friends I sometimes had sex with.

I tried to hate the world more than I hated Ashby. Like most humans, he had his own miles of mindfucking, self-mutilating experiences before I entered his life. However, one day in October, he proposed hanging out. I was at odds with how to do this, but I felt stronger than before, so I said sure, *why the fuck not?* But I asked Luis for advice that afternoon in the parlor.

"What are you doing this weekend?" I asked him, as he walked outside holding a lit spliff.

"I don't know, what are *you* doing this weekend?" Luis asked me, offering me a hit off the spliff.

"I don't know. I might hang out with someone. I don't know."

"Who? Oh girl, please don't."

"Why?"

"Fuck Ashby, he's a brainfuck. Oh dear. Oh dear. I didn't even know you still talked to him."

"We just talk sometimes. I can, however, see that he's too nice every now and then. It fucks with me. So I react. Question the gesture. Write a letter or two. Overanalyze. Then I smoke. Then I wish we could just talk in person. Act our age. Without games or manipulation. So I want to try. To act our age in person."

"You said it."

"What?"

"Manipulation."

"I know, I know, I should get over it, he's a dick. Blah. Luis, you are one motherly officer."

"I try."

"He keeps saying shit to make me feel as if he still wants me. He may well be doing that thing assholes do. Show love, when in reality they just want to fuck new cute girls. Or travel. Or be unemployed without anyone judging them. But they like the feeling of having you on their ass. So they egg it on. Personally, I enjoy traveling and fucking cute girls, but I have no ulterior motives. So, Luis, I think you might hate me. I'm aware of how abusive such a gesture is. But right now, I'm not even giving him shit for that."

"Why?"

"I don't know, reverse psychology. Maybe I'm an asshole too. Or maybe I'm too naïve and sympathetic over someone I shouldn't even be sympathetic about. Maybe I'm mistaking sympathy for attraction? The dude's got it rough now. But something in me wants to rehabilitate what's there, even just a friendship. I don't know."

"You're both crazy. You're both so crazy."

"I just keep asking him why he would do it. Why he would slip in kind gestures, knowing they keep me wanting him. Are we really destined to be great friends? I just want to, I don't know, have a discussion about it. I'm well aware he probably thinks I'm annoying or unattractive or some shit. You know. The typical reasons people dump people. But I know there's something, beyond the petty boy-girl-love bullshit, and I want to get there, because in theory we could be great creative, or even psychological partners.

And why the fuck would he conjure up this complex theory about some mysterious glitch disabling his capacity to fall in love with me—if he wanted to ultimately get rid of me? Come on. What a crazy thing to do. The only people who could openly and freely dissect their feelings like that to one another are those who make the best of friends, but terrible lovers. I don't know man. We gotta stop throwing each other away over dumb bullshit. There's too much legit bullshit out there making life more of this long impersonal road of nothing, 'cause no one can fucking talk to each other anymore."

I had smoked too much, and went off, aimlessly, on the past, present, and future: "I know he may have possibly used the whole 'I need to take care of my life' bullshit to cover a sensible need to just, I don't know, be single. Or at least be a gallivanting asshole without fear of persecution by a woman who knows him too well. Who fucking cares. I'm over it. He sucks at breaking up with people and that's that. I just, I don't know—I'm a weak piece of shit I guess. I don't know. I fucking miss him. And I'm accepting this plan to reconnect."

"No, it's fine. You talk to whoever you want. I'm sure there was more than just off-and-on romantic feelings. I believe that you connected in such a spiritually excellent way. I'm sure he was eating all of our food and eating all of our hallucinogenic mushrooms for something besides your pussy."

"Oh, shut up Luis. *Maldito come-mierda.*"

"Oh honey, you know I'm just fucking with you. I know you're just in love with him."

"Fuck you. Make me another burger."

*   *   *

That weekend, Ashby decided to pull me on a string, with consecutive dead end plans, resulting in my irrational accusations and whirlwind anger. Ashby and I bickered.

"If you don't want to hang out with me, I will not be hurt. Just fucking say so. Don't fucking say otherwise, dragging me along for the most dreadful ride of my life. You shit."

A painful bind over communication ended our long-distance interactions, until he would return to Brooklyn.

"I want to see you regularly when I move back," Ashby confessed as the fire settled into smoke.

"Yeah I'll hold you to that." Somewhat believing we were right souls at the wrong time, I didn't believe he would return, though I badly wanted him to. Occasionally I tried to believe those future plans, but more often, I tried to forget him altogether.

CHAPTER·NINETEEN

Predictable collapses
and the cost of freedom.

OCTOBER

The aroma of sewage had revisited the basement. Humidity had ceased for the last couple of months, until that Thursday afternoon, as a deadly winter interlaced with a summer gone harshly awry. Thursdays felt empty without Dust and we were all too nestled in our own interests and ambitions to throw parties. Wired from sixteen ounces of espresso, I walked past a baseball field in Greenpoint flooded with enthused teenagers laughing and chatting at recess. I was still paying rent by working at bars and writing stories, and I had very nice friends. *I have a pretty okay situation*, I reminded myself. I eased my fingers into the chain link fence and smiled a smile of jaded wisdom. If they only knew how much more fucked it'll get in ten years.

I looked up and saw the skyline of this city I sought as my true love when I moved here a year ago. She twinkled with despair and whispered *Destruction, rehabilitation, and revelation are my only constants. That's why we're a perfect pair, you and I.*

"I'm over being tormented by this. What the fuck have I missed in these two months?" I asked a woman who had sat beside me on a park bench, as we recited our love woes to one another. She had a face like porcelain and a tooth that was preciously chipped. She had on a flannel shirt over torn denim pants, ratty gray sneakers, and teased curls that I wanted to dive into. She smiled at I.

"Nothing's changed, I guess. It seems like the offbeat people still look as hot as they did fourteen years ago."

I took her telephone number. I never used it.

*   *   *

I was walking behind an attractive tattooed woman and a kid I assumed was her own. In intrepid envy, I wanted to hold the woman's hand. I walked beside her so I could smile at her. She rejected my smiling acknowledgement and I stopped walking.

A man was creeping out of a café's backdoor. He stopped beside me, and stared a discreetly fascinated stare. My eyes crossed his—they were the most perfect shade of pale blue and his head, the most perfect sphere—and I smiled but kept walking. He bored me. I sat on a park bench and the woman next to me looked concerned.

"Did you hear some plane just flew into a building in Manhattan? No one knows what it was all about," she recited.

"Damn that sucks," I consoled her. The destruction of physical structures reminded me that people will always burn one another in spite and competitive anguish. There are always two sides to a battle and whether one is right or both are wrong, the human condition will always malfunction in nature. And in a flurry of damp grace teetering on the edge of hopefulness, I faced the skyline.

"It's nice to see the Empire State Building from here. Who knows when there will be a puke green condo in the way," the woman said to me.

"Damn that Empire State Building. That bitch has made it far."

"'Cause her caretakers are rich-ass dudes."

"Ha. I hope I make it that far. Without the rich dudes."

"What about ass dudes?" I smiled at the woman and her wit made me a little wet.

*　　*　　*

FEBRUARY

Through the seasons, new lovers colonized my quixotic and sexually charged daydreaming. However, Ashby left occasional notes of loving, platonic interest, and eventually re-entered my life as a friend the next spring. His life was now polished, and I could see a distinct glare in his smile when we spoke in person for the first time after months.

We met in the afternoon at a diner. He held back from me, covered himself in a coat for a while, and I sat in my seat, feeling an awkward trepidation but also an enthusiasm I didn't really want to tell him about. We smoked cigarettes for anxiety, tiptoed around words that might release damp memories, and frolicked over our desires, thoughts, and newfangled ambitions. We shared our writing with one another, and it reminded me why all this shit was so hard. We entangled, in the same sense we did almost a year ago. The exchange at the diner tumbled into a second take at friendship. However, Ashby failed at being to me what a lost love would be to anyone else—a discarded memory with a new meaning. Because I still wanted Calvino Ashby. I just hid it well from myself when he wasn't around.

*   *   *

MARCH

Months later, during our second take at friendship, I confessed my feelings to him over a lengthy, hand-written letter. I expected rejection and painful, unequal sentiments to result in the typical diatribes that we still directed at one another. I might have debated whether I was still in love with him—or just the idea of him in a better light—and if I was really in love, or if I just wanted to fuck him. But his ability for brash honesty perished since my confession. I confessed so that we might stay friends, but Ashby never really responded, even for the sake of salvaging the precious connection between two once-amalgamated adults. The possibility of communication died with winter, and the last days of the cold lay bitterly beside me. We drifted, as I remained resentful for his failure to look me in the eye, like the friend he so adamantly claimed to want to be. Friendship, without processing my confession, would only torture me, for I had fallen in love with Calvino Ashby by mistake.

This time, for the first time, I set aside buses, trains, and rails of every variety. I let myself experience life while experiencing pain, without really overanalyzing the damage; I didn't think about where it made me wrong, but rather what I wanted to make right. From the bus stop to my front door, I walked home one afternoon, several days after administering my confession. I puffed succulent illegality and wondered when the post office was closing. I looked forward to having dinner that day, and marveled kindly at the sunlight I had recently missed out on. Children were laughing outside and it made me happy. This was where inner change started, I deduced. Not in shameless self-criticism, but rather in shutting up, living, and somehow, metaphysically, achieving.

*   *   *

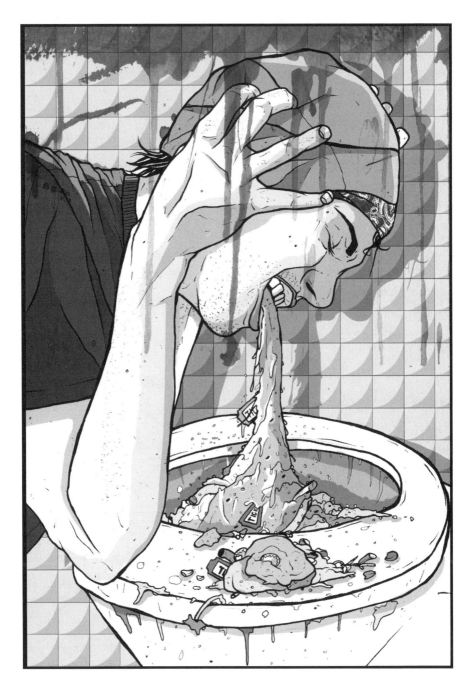

CHAPTER TWENTY

This stick in my ass
is part of growing up.

"That's just what men do," my mother commented on Ashby's behavior, as did Rhonda, my next-door neighbor Aline, and the woman who worked at the laundromat to whom I often verbally vomited my romantic woes.

I wasn't dumb. I was well aware the cold shoulder was a common reaction to emotional intensity, especially, in my experience, for straight men. And while a lot of people in my life accepted this method of breaking up, I decided to fight it. Although I understood and sympathized with it, for I had already sulked in utter bewilderment after writing long, aggressive letters and yelling over the telephone. I, too, was exhausted.

Why can't one realize a face-to-face interaction will validate the importance of a friendship whose future is at stake, whether or not anything fucking happens? Whether or not we decide to hate each other? I would ask myself, as the edge of my psychological sword became dull. I didn't believe physical interaction could save the dead romance between Ashby and me. I just felt it could, somehow, remind us that what once was, still carried a sense of importance in both our lives—and the end should be treated with as much tender care as the beginning.

However, the silent treatment, experienced by many people in unbalanced relationships between poor communicators, once again pulsated through my annoying little life. But hell, I was used to it. I didn't feel that suspected sense of worthlessness, I just felt annoyed, irritated by how difficult it was for someone to tap on a little glitch in their system, and, for once, make me feel as if I'm important enough to them that they would want to look me in the eye as they speak the utter truth. But hardly feeling like a failure, I accepted the fact that changing the socialization of an ex-lover could be a dead-end quest, and I'd rather not die trying.

*   *   *

Later that spring, I asked Spike to meet me in Coney Island on the first warm day of the year. I had heard Coney Island might be torn down the next year. I tried my hardest to take loving advantage of what was left of her, before every festive corner of New York City disappeared, leaving traces of dead amusement parks that I only enjoyed with dead love. Spike and I faced the water.

Spike peered over to a man by a trashcan. "That guy totally has something in his ass, and he can't stop picking it. Ha."

"Ugh. That man reminds me so much of Ashby."

A man in a blue bandana leaning against a trashcan scratched his ass crack for a minute, which in my subconscious lasted a year. "That kid killed me, man," I mused to Spike.

"Yeah, but you don't need that. Don't even sweat it. That kid fell off his rocker long before he met you. Here, smoke more, fuck Ashby. Don't reminisce." Spike rehabilitated my spirit. I took a hit and smiled a smile of uncanny proportions.

"We admitted shit to each other that most people in their right minds would hide from their lovers. It's not like we just did coke, fucked, and I overanalyzed the destructive conclusion."

"Like you did with Smith?"

"Ha. Yeah." I sunk in embarrassment and laughed for a second. "I was as honest as I fucking could be. And he just *had* to be a fucking coward. I don't want him to love me. I want him to treat me like a person. Never once did I persecute him for not wanting me."

"Never."

"I just wanted, I don't know, an ending with dignity."

"Vent. I'm refueling." Spike packed a bowl into a translucent one-hitter and held it to his face, fighting the fury of the wind.

"It just sucks that my honesty, this time around, had to go out the same fucking way it did in the beginning. Is it that fucking difficult to tell the truth to some girl's face?"

"Hell if I know. I don't even date them."

"Like, 'Car. I haven't redeveloped an urge to bone, as you so peculiarly have, so tell me your boundaries, and I'll respect them. I want to be your friend. Because I supposedly care about you.' I mean, seriously. What a fucking shit-for-brains. What is so hard about that?"

"Don't have a fucking clue. Here have another hit off this loaded, plastic cigarette."

"I don't know man. It's not like I think he's it. For a minute, he did seem like everything, like when we were in the same room. Of course, lately, I've learned that he's just a, I don't know—*another dude*. And I get over it. But then I see that guy. That guy scratching his ass by the motherfucking trash can and I remember how nice it was that one time he wasn't another dude."

"Yo, remember last weekend when you finally made out with what's-her-face with the fucking hair? And the gigantic head? You love that shit.

You got game, girl. You only keep going back to that Ashby-sentimentality 'cause he's the last lover you really cared about. But this is good. This end where you vent and smoke and rage.'"

"Yeah. Ugh." I took a hit and sighed. "I guess I just wish my urge to fuck everyone wasn't such a catalyst for the destruction of a friendship."

"Yeah. Totally."

For the first time, on that boardwalk with Spike, I really believed in that kind of love, whether it existed flawlessly or in shambles. I felt free. Maryjane was quick like a rabbit, and Spike was my true redeemer. Suddenly, love seemed delightful and possible, just unnecessary at the moment.

"Girl, just get on your vibrator, ride hard, and forget what people say," Spike assured me of a prosperous future between sexuality and myself.

"Really," I paused. "Yo, do you want to go get an ice cream? I forgot what we were talking about."

"Yeah, I totally want an ice cream."

A new season filtered through the same Brooklyn. I flicked the ash of a wilted Black & Mild cigarillo while I reaped the dearest benefits of the windswept memory of Calvino Ashby. That afternoon, on a wooden board-walk bench hovering over shifty planks, Spike fidgeted with a broken guitar and I licked my lips.

"What's done is done and may what looms be well," I said, puffing a ring of smoke into the air. "But I will never forget that fucking bitch."

CHAPTER TWENTY-ONE

Benediction and a beer.

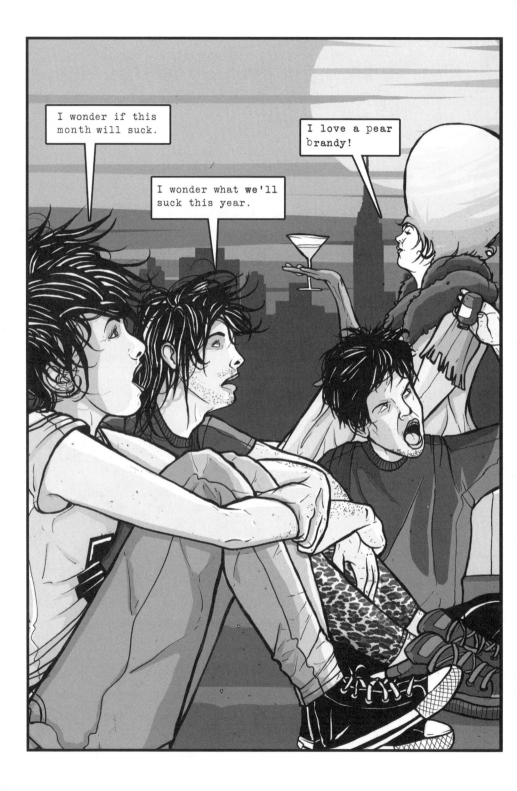

JULY

The existing threats to dismantle Coney Island were averted for another span of time, and another season of Astroland was declared on that July. For a few more months, 300 Astroland employees had jobs on a battleground whose rent was escalating to several million more dollars a month.

So the next year, again, would be quite possibly the last for Astroland, the Cyclone, and the assorted odds and ends of humanity offering sausage, french fries, clown makeup, and dilapidated beach castles adorned in the most perfect rainbow color schemes. New York City was fragile and threatened in all the same ways since the beginning of time. We humans, however, are just eternally suffocated by that damned threat of pain and misfortune. And in the meantime, we finally were good enough to make the best of it. That July, our entire house moved out of the Palace beneath the Brooklyn–Queens Expressway into a neighborhood with more trees. The green of the leaves, the rustic street lamps, historically preserved brownstones, and the people's voices running in and out of earshot as I walked down the street created a neighborhood that could give birth to another revelatory year.

On the steps of my new house, I looked back at my entrance into New York City and remembered Dust. I remembered how RJ, Luis, Spike, and I were at odds with the world because one day we realized we were *different*. This move, however, entailed a new, deeper understanding of the vicious romance between love and pain. Because without pain, I couldn't appreciate love, and without love, my soul wilted into rubble. Sex just doesn't always have to accompany love; unlike the byproduct that pain is, love and sex can exist happily independent from one another.

Huddled in a corner of a dive on 5TH Avenue in Brooklyn, Spike and I licked the savory rims of afternoon margaritas. Spike was working on a new song and I was writing something about saints, virgins, and how Isabelle, that psychic I had visited over a year ago, wasn't as wrong as I presumed. A woman walked through the door in a knee-length skirt and oversized bejeweled sunglasses. She looked lost and adorable, with a generously sized wooden board pressed between her arm and ribcage. I asked her to come over, so I could look at it. The colors reminded me of my favorite book as a kid, about a jungle with alien inhabitants who had peculiar, possibly unintentional, human anatomy. I adored the art of '80s science fiction children's literature and I adored her walk and the tattooed script on her left calf. Spike applauded my discovery and I salivated at the thought of her beginning to clutch her chapped lips around a glass of dazzling yellow beer. She walked towards us and tilted her head in a bemused curiosity, as I complimented her painting, which she evidently created herself.

"I've met you before." Revealed from behind the plastic shades was the face of Sally Hackett, my one-night German love.

"Oh shit, it's nice to see you. And your paintings. It's nice to see you're well. And you know, painting."

"Yeah totally."

"It looks nice. I like the trees." While the trees looked a little too vaginal, my interest in her left me frail as my cheeks became blushed.

"Thank you."

"No problem. Take a chair." Sally sat at our table and for several minutes we lamented on criminal justice and drugs at nightclubs. Sally was thinking of attending law school, while many of my friends' places of work were being groundlessly raided.

"And when I become the bomb-ass lawyer of New York City, no gay bar will ever experience the absurdity of unfounded persecution ever again!" Sally was a relatively excited person.

"I'm happy for you," I lauded her, and we talked about my stint with high school teaching and she laughed, kindly. "I'm just too crazy. So I'm just a writer now."

"*Just* a writer? Honey, don't disparage yourself so blindly."

"Oh, Sally."

"Oh shit, it's been an hour when I said it'd be a minute, I have to go."

"Well, it was nice to run into you."

"Stop by Clancy's on C and 4TH Street. I work there."

"Totally. I'd like to actually talk to you more," I obliged, with sincerity.

"Yeah definitely. It was nice running into you again."

"It's nicer you remember me."

"Oh girl, those were wild times," Sally said as she walked away.

"Those were the good old days," I yelled in her direction, as she exited the rear door.

"Ha. The good old days of being self-righteous slobs," Spike said.

"Yeah. But at least we were good at being slobs. Destructive, excitable, soul-searching slobs."

"Totally. And what's the point of being a slob if you're not getting fucked up all the time?" Spike laughed at the past's scuffles, and I did too.

*   *   *

The good old days trundled through summer as a distant memory that still surfaced every so often. Life offers the opportunity for debauchery every couple of years, and to some, every couple of days. I looked back at that year of malevolent heartache gripping the limbs of outstanding euphoria, giving birth to yet another chapter. Spike laughed when I reminded him that that was the girl who nearly bit off my nipple after that one New Year's Eve at Dick's.

"The good old days. That is wild," Spike lamented. "I guess those were the good old days, alright."

"Yeah. If only someone would have told us at the time."

ABOUT THE AUTHOR

Cristy C. Road is a freelance illustrator, 'zine publisher, and writer. She lives in Brooklyn, New York.

PHOTO BY AMOS MAC

ACKNOWLEDGMENTS

Thanks to my family, for letting me be somewhat of a freak. To Michelle Proffit for editing this and being the first to make any sense of it. To Holly Bemiss for making me realize change doesn't mean selling out. To all of my friends that have ever given a fuck about me, everyone who let me draw them, and all the people who make New York City a nice place to live: Tommy Hottpants, Carolanne Marcantonio, Ben Haber, Gabriel Defazio, Sasha Gilbert Wortzel, Tom-Tom, Duch, Steve, Casey, Microcosm Publishing, Lauren Denitzio, Josh, Pat, Randee, Codee, Stephen, Haley, Rachelle, Rashaun, Sara, Crystal Bradley, Jon, all the nice people at Soft Skull, and Colleen and Aimee Jennings for convincing me to move here in the first place. To Michelle Tea, Rhiannon Argo, Nicole Georges, Ali Liebegott, Annie Oakley, Eileen Myles, Tamara Llosa Sandor, and Robin Akimbo for the Sister Spit Tour. To my favorite writers, my favorite bands, and anyone else who sort of changed my life forever.